Crimson Harvest

Ken Sandoval

CRIMSON HARVEST

First edition. April 28, 2024.

ISBN: 979-8224300327

Written by Ken Sandoval.

Chapter One

A bitter wind howled over the desolate moor, whipping Ingram Brown's long coat around his legs as he trekked the rutted dirt road into the village of Sableford. In the fading light of dusk, he made out the silhouettes of decrepit buildings huddled together as if for warmth and protection. Their sagging frames cast deep shadows in the dying light speaking of hard lives etched by toil and poverty.

Approaching the first house, Ingram raised a gloved hand to rap sharply on the weathered door. He stepped back, the worn leather of his boots creaking in the silence as he waited for signs of life within. After a long moment, a slat slid open, and a pair of eyes peered out suspiciously.

"What business have ye here, stranger?" rasped a voice from inside.

"I intend to take a room at the inn for the season," Ingram replied. "Name's Ingram Brown."

The eyes sized him up. "No one passes through here in winter," the voice muttered. "Are you a peddler?"

Ingram met the gaze steadily. "My business is my own. If you'll point me toward the inn, I'll trouble you no further."

The gruff voice replied, "The Black Boar inn lies just beyond the church up the road," and the man promptly closed the slat with a decisive thud. Ingram sighed, his breath pluming in the frozen air, and adjusted the pack on his broad shoulders. Clearly the villagers in this remote outpost wanted no dealings with outsiders. But Ingram's purpose here went beyond their distrustful nature. An ancient evil stalked this land, and he aimed to root it out.

Trudging onwards, Ingram scanned the buildings that lined the narrow lane. Oil lamps glowed dimly behind cracked windows, but he spotted no figures braving the bitter cold outside. At the end of the lane, the silhouette of a steepled church stood out starkly against the night sky. His destination lay just beyond.

Rounding a bend, Ingram spotted the wooden sign of the Black Boar Inn hanging above a heavy oak door, its iron brackets worn thin with age. Stomping the snow from his boots, he pushed inside.

The gloomy interior was lit only by the hearth's struggling fire and a few candles stubbed low in their sconces. A tall old man stood behind the bar, drying glasses with a dingy rag. At Ingram's entrance, what few patrons were present fell silent, eyeing him with undisguised suspicion.

Ingram approached the barman. "I require lodging for the season. I'm told you have a room."

The old man frowned, sizing him up. "We don't see your sort here often," he remarked. Ingram remained silent under the scrutiny until the man shrugged and retrieved a key. "Room's at the top of the stairs. We start meals at sunrise and finish 'fore full dark. Don't want no wandering about once the sun sets. Best mind your own business if ye wish to survive the winter."

Ingram's lips tightened. "My thanks," he replied, taking the offered key. His eyes swept the shadowed room as he turned toward the stairs. The villagers studiously avoided his gaze, murmuring in low voices and making signs against evil. Ingram's shoulders tensed beneath his coat. So, the darkness plaguing this village had sunk its claws in deep. All the more reason for him to see his task through, no matter the cost.

Ingram nodded briefly at the suspicious-looking patrons as he crossed the dim common room. His boots clomped up the creaky wooden stairs to the small room he had rented. After taking off his coat, he fell onto the lumpy straw mattress. After so many miles, he was completely drained. His eyelids grew heavy almost instantly. In just a few moments he was asleep, temporarily free from worries about his trip.

Ingram awoke just before sunrise, the pale light of dawn filtering through the room's dirty window. He had slept little, dreams haunted by the cries of those already lost to the evil he hunted. Rising, he knelt beside the bed to murmur the prayers that focused his resolve. Though his enemies were godless abominations, Ingram knew his own soul must remain pure for God's divine justice to flow through him. Only diligent prayer and meditation could keep the creeping doubts at bay.

Belting on his coat, Ingram tucked a rosary into his pocket and slung his pack of wooden spikes carved with holy symbols over one broad shoulder. Thus, armed, he made his way downstairs to break his fast. The common room was empty save for the barman, already wiping down tables by the pale light of morning. He glared at Ingram but said nothing as he served some steaming hot porridge cooking before the battered hearth.

Ingram ate quickly then ventured outside to get his bearings. The village by daylight seemed shrunken, as if the night swelled its proportions with the evil it hid. What few villagers he saw scurried quickly about their business, heads down. Disease and poverty had taken their toll here.

Wandering the town's single muddy lane, Ingram nodded greetings but received only furtive glances in return. At the church, he found the doors barred shut with heavy planks. The attached cemetery had a new grave that bore only a simple wooden marker.

Pausing, Ingram recited a quick prayer for the nameless soul. Too many fresh graves of late if the murmurs he'd overheard last night held any truth. And he had no doubt they did. The valleys and peaks surrounding this remote village had long been stalking grounds for all manner of demon. But the creatures he sought would not be laid to rest easily.

By mid-morning, Ingram found himself approaching a tidy homestead on the village outskirts. The cozy structure appeared to be in better repair than its neighbors, with glass panes intact and smoke wisping from the chimney. As Ingram drew near, the front door opened, and a woman emerged carrying a bucket.

She paused at the sight of him, the wind catching strands of her long auburn hair. Though she wore a guarded expression, Ingram sensed warmth beneath her reserve. He inclined his head. "Good morrow to you, miss. I'm Ingram Brown, newly arrived in your village. And whom might I have the pleasure of addressing?"

The woman studied him a moment, pale blue eyes considering. "I'm Shannon Johnston," she finally replied. "This be my family's farm, or what's left of it."

Ingram's dark eyebrows rose. "You tend it alone then?"

Shannon resumed walking toward the barn, gesturing for him to follow. "Since my father died, I look after my sister Dana as best I can. But the land grows stubborn, and the livestock sickly of late."

"My condolences for your father," Ingram offered. "No doubt many hands make lighter work of a farmstead. Should you require assistance, I would be glad to aid you."

A slight smile touched Shannon's wind-chapped lips. "You're either very kind or very new to these parts if you'd take work from the likes of me."

Before Ingram could ask her meaning, Shannon turned and smiled, eyes on the path ahead. Following her gaze, Ingram saw a hulking figure approaching, axe resting on one broad shoulder. Though the man's bearded jaw was tense, Ingram read kindness in his flinty eyes.

Letting the axe head drop to the ground with a thud, the man nodded to Shannon then fixed Ingram with a searching look. "You're the stranger come to stay, then?" At Ingram's nod, he thrust out a calloused hand. "Walter Daniels. I've the farm next over."

Ingram clasped Walter's strong grip. "Ingram Brown. Well met, Walter."

Releasing his hand, Walter squinted at the brightening sky. "Best we all get to our chores 'fore full light. Work enough for two men on each farm hereabouts, yet all are short hands."

He held Ingram's gaze meaningfully. "Some hands being colder than others, if you take my meaning."

Ingram's eyes narrowed, but Walter had already hefted his axe and turned towards his own land. Shannon avoided Ingram's questioning look. "I should see to my sister," she murmured before hurrying towards the house.

Ingram watched her go, unease prickling his spine. There was more troubling this village than impoverished crops and sickly animals. An ancient evil festered in this isolated valley, draining life and hope from its people. And though they feared to speak of it, Ingram aimed to drag it into the merciless light of God.

The day passed swiftly as Ingram explored the surrounding valleys and peaks on foot, orienting himself to the rugged landscape that sheltered the village. Little stirred in these desolate highlands save ragged crows and a lone hawk riding bitter winds above barren ridges. The stillness felt heavy, filled with unseen watching eyes.

Descending into the forested valley as dusk fell, Ingram found it eerily silent. Not even the wind penetrated the dense pine boughs. A hastily marked trail showed where timber had recently been felled, perhaps to shore up the dilapidated village buildings. Emerging from the trees, Ingram spotted a hunched figure making slow but steady progress bundles of firewood balanced on its shoulders.

As he drew nearer, the figure straightened, revealing herself to be an elderly woman, her gnarled hands and stooped shoulders attesting to a lifetime of hard labor. Though her lined face bore a stern expression, Ingram detected wisdom and resilience in the depths of her dark eyes.

"Let me carry that burden for you, grandmother," he offered, reaching to take the firewood from her thin shoulders.

The old woman shrank back, shaking her head vehemently. "I'll not have your help, Hunter, nor will any here," she rasped, pulling her faded shawl tighter.

Ingram froze mid-gesture, eyes narrowing. "How do you name me Hunter?" he asked carefully.

The crone peered at him. "Darkness knows its own bane. But your fight's not ours. Leave this place."

Before Ingram could respond, she scurried away surprisingly quickly, muttering under her breath. Brow furrowed, he watched her disappear into the gloom between the sagging buildings. How had she divined his true purpose here? If others held similar knowledge, his task could be gravely complicated.

Shaking off the unease her words provoked, Ingram returned to the inn as heavy dusk settled over the valley. He ate a thin stew before the hearth then retired to his cramped chamber to prepare his weapons. If evil stalked these lands, he would meet it with faith and sharpened wood.

Chapter Two

Midnight approached as Ingram knelt by the room's narrow window, murmuring prayers of protection and will. The village lay still, not even dogs barking to break the oppressive silence. His meditations complete, Ingram was reaching for his coat when a bloodcurdling scream tore through the darkness.

Ingram froze, hand on his rosary. Then he seized his stakes and raced downstairs, the scream's echo still ringing in his ears. Bursting outside into the moonless night, he strained his senses for the source. Again, the scream came, this time seeming nearby. Ingram outpaced his racing heart towards the sound. If someone was in the clutches of the evil he'd sensed, there was not a moment to lose.

Rounding a decrepit barn, Ingram stumbled to a halt. Beneath the looming pines, he glimpsed a figure bent over a woman's prone form. By her swirling skirts and the gleam of auburn hair, Ingram recognized Shannon, though her face was obscured by the shadowed form above her.

Ingram's fist tightened on a stake as his pulse roared in his ears. "Release her, hell spawn!" he roared, brandishing the carved wood.

The figure spun with an unnatural hiss, eyes glowing red in the darkness. Ingram glimpsed the flash of white fangs before the creature vanished, blending into the shadows between one heartbeat and the next.

Ingram stood ready until certain the threat had passed. Then he raced to Shannon's side. Her neck was bloodied, skirt torn and limbs sprawled awkwardly in the dirt of the barnyard. But shallow breaths still moved her chest, proving she yet clung to life.

Gently gathering her limp form, Ingram carried Shannon inside, kicking open the farmhouse door and striding to the hearth. As he laid her down, Dana appeared from the back room, freezing at the sight before her. She shared Shannon's auburn hair but had a youthful innocence in her wide eyes that her sister's harder life had stripped away.

"Bandages," Ingram commanded. "And any medicines you have."

Dana blinked as if confused before Ingram's sharp tone spurred her to action. As she gathered the requested items, Ingram found a clean cloth and began gently washing the blood from Shannon's neck. Though his hands were calloused from combat, he cleaned her wound as tenderly as a father with a babe.

Shannon soon moaned softly, her eyes fluttering open. They widened at the sight of the stranger leaning over her, and she tried to raise herself up.

"Hush," Ingram soothed. "You are gravely hurt but safe now." At his words, Shannon's body relaxed, though her eyes remained bewildered and frightened. Ingram continued gently tending her wound as her sister returned with bandages and two small bottles.

Working together, they treated and dressed Shannon's injury. Once finished, Ingram carried her to her bed, where she immediately slipped back into a restless sleep. Dana hovered worriedly until Ingram convinced her to try resting while he kept watch.

Alone with the sleeping Shannon, Ingram added a log to the struggling fire then settled into a chair to wait out the night. But sleep eluded him as his mind churned over what he'd glimpsed in the darkness.

The creature had moved with unnatural speed, vanishing like mist on the wind. Its eyes had glowed with an infernal hunger that chilled Ingram's battle-hardened soul. His fist clenched on his rosary at the memory. There was no longer any doubt; this village was in the grip of vampires. And the poor souls trapped here were helpless against their demonic power.

Ingram gazed at Shannon's restless slumber. She had survived this attack but borne a grievous wound. There would be others less fortunate if the number of fresh graves were any indication. This village and its people cried out for deliverance. Ingram had answered that call. He would not rest until the servants of darkness plaguing this land were returned to the hell that spawned them.

Sunrise brought a heavy knocking at the farmhouse door. Ingram opened it to find Walter and a woman filling the entry, axe in hand and brow carved with worry. At the sight of Ingram, his craggy face creased in confusion then suspicion. Ingram raised a forestalling hand.

"She lives. Though gravely wounded, Shannon rests."

Walter's massive shoulders slumped in relief. He stepped inside, gently laying the axe down before going to kneel by his unconscious neighbor. Shannon's sister emerged from the back room, her wan face and reddened eyes attesting to her sleepless vigil.

"How came she to be hurt on our very threshold?" Walter demanded, though it seemed he already suspected the truth. Jaw tightening, Ingram chose his words with care.

"I know not what evil has stalked your village of late, but it struck Shannon last eve before fleeing at my arrival." He held Walter's shrewd gaze. "I mean to see this threat rooted out, but I must know what darkness you people have invited into your midst."

Walter's eyes bored into Ingram's, weighing his measure. Then the stoic man bowed his head. "It is as I feared then. The crimson harvest begins anew."

Before Ingram could ask his meaning, a low moan drew all eyes to the bed. Shannon was stirring, her eyelids finally fluttering open. She shrank back at the sight of the four figures looming over her, panic flashing.

Ingram quickly knelt beside the bed. "Take ease, Shannon. Only friends surround you."

Slowly her panic receded, replaced by confusion. "What...what happened?" she whispered. "I remember the barn...such cold..." She shuddered, tears welling in her eyes.

"Dwell not on it for now," Ingram soothed, though inwardly he burned to confirm the nature of her attack. "Rest and recover your strength."

Shannon's eyes focused on his, clarity returning. "You saved me," she murmured. "I heard your shout and for a moment hoped..." She trailed off, fresh tears spilling down her pale cheeks.

Ingram hesitated, then placed a reassuring hand on hers. "We shall speak of this when you are healed. But know evil did not claim you last eve, nor shall I allow it to find you again."

Shannon searched his face through her tears, then nodded weakly. Settling back, she slipped again into a restless sleep. Ingram watched her for a moment, silent resolve hardening his visage. Then he rose and turned to Walter, whose shrewd eyes had missed nothing.

"Speak your mind plainly, man," Ingram demanded. "What evil has gripped your people?"

Walter held his measuring look a moment longer, then nodded slowly. "Very well. But not here." He glanced at his wife, who was wringing her hands by the bedside. "Mary, keep a close watch on her. We shall return shortly."

She blinked nervously but bobbed her head in acceptance. Walter led Ingram outside into the pale morning light. They entered the musty and dim barn. Walter paused to stroke the muzzle of a dappled mare who whinnied softly at his presence. Then he turned to face Ingram, his rugged features etched with a grim expression.

"The evil that stole upon my neighbor has haunted these valleys since mortal memory," he began. "My forefathers whispered of those who shun the sun, preying upon lost souls straying too far from the hearth fire's glow. Creatures who steal your very lifeblood to prolong their unnatural existence." His brows drew down darkly. "Vrykolakas, we called them in my grandfather's time."

Despite himself, Ingram drew a sharp breath. "Blood drinkers," he muttered. "It is as I feared."

Walter nodded grimly. "They ever lurk in shadowed places, emerging to feed when their numbers grow too great." He clenched a fist. "Then it is the crimson harvest, when not a soul is safe and all live in dread. We fortify our homes and do not wander after night falls. But still people vanish on occasion, only to resurface later as one of the soulless creatures themselves. It is a terror from the old times come again."

He shook his head sadly. "My own Mother perished in such a harvest when I was but a boy. She went out to draw water from the well one evening and never returned. Two nights later we found her standing motionless outside our door, skin white as the moon, eyes glowing crimson with unholy hunger. My father knew what she had become and did what had to be done, though it broke his heart."

Walter fell silent, reliving the painful memory. Then he met Ingram's gaze steadily. "So, you see, the true horror of these demons is not merely the loss of life, but the loss of kin and soul. "Since then, the creatures kept their distance, and our vigilance waned. But now, too many like Shannon have been lost to the night. Fresh graves appear weekly, but none dare speak of it. Old charms and wards go neglected. If left unchecked, soon none of us will survive to see spring's thaw. Death comes for us all in time. But to become an abomination, cursed to prey upon your own..." He trailed off with a shudder.

"We must stop the spread of this evil before more innocents are lost," Ingram agreed grimly. He tightened his grip on the stake carved with ancient symbols. "By God's grace, we shall purge these lands of their cursed influence."

His peace said, Walter fell silent, watching Ingram closely.

Ingram met his gaze with fire in his eyes. "Your people have suffered much, but suffer no longer," he declared. "God has guided my steps here just as the sun begins to fade. I know these creatures well and have devoted my life to destroying their unholy kind."

He drew a stake carved with crosses and ancient sigils from his coat. "Place your trust in me, and I vow upon my mortal soul every last demon shall be cleansed from these lands."

Walter studied the stake and the iron-clad conviction in Ingram's eyes. Slowly, he nodded.

"Very well, Hunter. The villages' fate rests in your hands now. Without Shannon, my Mary cannot run our farm alone. I will aid you as I am able." He gripped Ingram's shoulder with a work-roughened hand. "Beware, the beasts are cunning and will not easily be rooted from their roosts."

Ingram's lips tightened. "I shall find them wherever they hide and pull them into the light of God."

Glancing outside at the climbing sun, Walter nodded grimly. "Come. There are preparations to make before dusk."

Ingram followed him from the barn, purpose fueling his steps. As they crossed the farmyard, he cast a silent prayer heavenward.

God, grant me the strength and wisdom for the battle ahead. The villagers' lives hang in the balance. With faith as my sword and your grace as my shield, I shall send these abominations back to the hell that spawned them.

Squaring his shoulders, Ingram strode after Walter to begin laying plans for the coming night's hunt. If any servants of darkness roamed these lands, he would find them.

Chapter Three

As the sun sank below the barren ridgeline, shadows crept through the ravines and hollows surrounding the remote village. A bitter wind wailed between the decrepit buildings, sending drifts of snow swirling down the deserted lane. Not a soul stirred outside in the deepening gloom.

Inside the dim confines of the inn, Ingram sat by the sputtering hearth, ignoring the sidelong glances from the withdrawn villagers who huddled over their meals. His dark gaze was turned inward, meditating on the best tactics for the coming night's hunt. Walter entered, stomping the snow from his boots, and joined Ingram at the table.

"All is prepared," Walter muttered under his breath. "I secured some charms from Old Miriam on the edge of the forest. Eccentric woman, but none alive know more of the old ways than she."

Ingram nodded, examining the crude fetishes and sigils Walter produced from his pockets. "We may need her lore before this is through. For now, let us see what secrets the darkness holds."

Belting on their stakes and charms, the two men departed into the snow-shrouded streets. Ingram paused outside the church, its imposing edifice now grim and unwelcoming with boarded windows and a stout plank barring the doors. What forces kept the frightened villagers from seeking sanctuary within? Ingram's jaw tightened as he whispered a brief prayer, then turned to follow Walter towards the forest.

The village of Sableford ended abruptly at the tree line, beyond which the track dwindled to a narrow, overgrown path. The bare limbs of the forest closed above them, muting the bitter wind. An unnatural stillness permeated the woods, as if all living things shunned this place after nightfall. Ingram's senses strained for any sign of movement in the gloom between the trees. But only their muted footfalls and the whisper of falling snow sounded beneath the silent pines.

The further they delved under the forest's eaves; the stronger Ingram's sense of apprehension grew. Unseen eyes seemed to track their progress from the concealing shadows. Twice he glimpsed a pale form flitting between the trees ahead, only to find nothing there when they gave pursuit. The very air felt heavy with watchful malice.

"They know we hunt them," Ingram murmured. Walter nodded grimly, axe and charms at the ready. But the preternatural creatures kept their distance, never presenting the two men a target for their sharpened stakes.

Frustration mounting, Ingram called a halt in a moonlit clearing. "We are no nearer finding their lair than when we began," he admitted. "They hold all the advantages here."

"Perhaps we should..." Walter began before cutting off, head cocked. Then Ingram heard it too; a distant shriek that curdled the blood. It echoed through the silent forest before being swallowed by the snow-laden boughs.

Immediately Ingram sprinted towards the sound, weaving between the trees as fast as his legs could carry him. The unearthly cry came twice more, each time closer. Bursting from the tree line, Ingram skidded to a halt, his boiling blood turning to ice.

There, against the stark white snow, lay a figure pinned beneath a hulking, monstrous shape. Dead eyes stared lifelessly up at the sky as the creature savaged its prey with awful hunger. Ingram seized a stake inscribed with holy symbols.

"Face me, fiend!" he roared, brandishing the sacred weapon. With unnatural speed, the demonic beast spun to face this new threat, blood smearing its pale features. Eyes burning crimson locked with Ingram's, and it bared jagged fangs in a vicious snarl. Then it was gone, melting into the darkness between one heartbeat and the next.

Ingram held his ground, senses straining for any sign the creature still lurked nearby. When several frozen minutes passed with no movement save the falling snow, he hurried to the victim's side. Though he knew it was too late, he felt for a pulse at the ravaged throat. The man's skin was already turning cold, all life fled from his brutally mauled form.

Walter panted up, axe ready, and surveyed the grisly scene with a muttered oath. "Poor Jonah. He just joined as night watchman." Walter shook his head sadly. "Never stood a chance against one of them."

With an effort, Ingram fought down his boiling rage over this loss of innocent life. Such raw emotion would only cloud his focus. He must remain vigilant and turn the seething hatred into an instrument of divine justice.

"We cannot leave him here to rise again tomorrow eve," Ingram said roughly, the words bitter ashes in his mouth. Together he and Walter gathered the broken body and carried it back through the silent woods. They would need to arrange a hasty funeral come morning and keep watch through the day to ensure Jonah did not reawaken as an abomination. It was a heavy burden, but all Ingram could do for now was to preserve the remnants of his soul.

Trudging back into the village, the two men took turns keeping solemn watch over the corpse until exhaustion claimed them both. But sleep brought Ingram little rest. His dreams seethed with horrific images of the poor souls claimed by this evil, their humanity shredded away. He awoke before dawn, jaw clenched. Payment was coming due for every drop of innocent blood. And Ingram aimed to be the hand that imposed God's justice.

Morning brought pale gray light filtering over the landscape of snow-draped rooftops and empty streets. Walter set off to inform the next of kin and arrange the funeral while Ingram stood guard over Jonah's remains. The day passed slowly, villagers emerging to clear paths and tend livestock, but all avoided the small cottage serving as a makeshift morgue.

As dusk approached, a humble procession approached bearing a plain wooden coffin. Walter and three other men carried the box down the lane in somber silence. Ingram murmured a brief prayer over Jonah before helping load the coffin. The men hauled their grim burden to the churchyard as the sky darkened above the peaks.

After the abbreviated funeral, the villagers quickly dispersed to the safety of their homes. Soon the streets were empty save for Ingram and Walter surveying the fresh plot.

"That others may yet escape his fate, we must find the lair of these demons tonight," Ingram said grimly. Walter nodded, his craggy face etched with fatigue that mirrored Ingram's own.

But they could not afford to delay. The pale moon rose, spilling its cold radiance over the abandoned streets. Tonight, the hunt would begin in earnest.

Chapter Four

Ingram waited until full darkness enveloped the village before slipping outside into the icy night. Above, clouds scudded across the blade of a crescent moon, plunging the landscape into fitful shadow. He moved silently between inky pools of blackness, senses straining for hidden watchers. At the edge of town, he met Walter, who was emerging from behind a vacant smithy with an axe and charms in hand. Ingram gave a nod of greeting before turning towards the forest.

The trail soon disappeared beneath wind-sculpted drifts of snow. Ingram followed the remembered way, moving as noiselessly as possible over the frozen ground. The cold air stung his lungs with each breath, sending plumes of vapor into the silent woods. He and Walter spoke no word, mutually wary of alerting the creatures to their presence.

When the trees thinned ahead, Ingram signaled a halt. Here he and Walter had recovered poor Jonah's ravaged corpse just yesterday morning. No signs marked the site now, the trampled snow already obscured by fresh powder. But Ingram recalled the location once hallowed ground that he would reclaim from evil. Kneeling, he pulled a small flask of holy water from inside his coat and poured a few drops on the perfect white expanse. "May God bless this land and cleanse it of all wickedness and impurity," he intoned under his breath. The water froze instantly but lingered as a tangible reminder of his oath.

Rising, Ingram led the way deeper into the woods. If the demons fed along the forest's edge, surely their lair must reside at its heart. He strained every sense trying to pierce the darkness shrouding their path. But no trace or spoor hinted at the passing of unearthly feet. The silent boughs yielded up no secrets.

Frustration mounting, Ingram called a halt in a moonlit glade. "I cannot pick up their trail," he admitted. "It is as if they simply materialize from shadow itself."

"Could the legends be true then?" Walter rumbled. "That they can change to a bat, a wolf or mist and vanish on the wind?" His naturally stoic face showed traces of unease at the thought.

Ingram's jaw tightened. "No being gifted by God, no matter how corrupted, can defy His natural laws in such a manner," he asserted. Walter looked unconvinced.

"Come. Let us..." Ingram broke off at Walter's abrupt gesture for silence. The big man tilted his head, listening intently. Then Ingram heard it too, a faint rustling that seemed to echo strangely between the trees ahead. He locked eyes with Walter, who gave a grim nod. Gripping their weapons, they moved stealthily towards the sounds, which slowly resolved into voices murmuring just above the edge of hearing.

Pausing behind the massive trunk of an ancient fir, Ingram peered ahead. Through a screen of snow-laden boughs he at first saw nothing. Then a flicker of movement drew his eyes to strange shadows cast against the white drifts. He realized an outcropping of weathered stones rose ahead, near enough to the trees to form a sheltered hollow. And by the unnatural silhouette, something lurked within that recess.

Ingram turned to Walter and gestured that he would circle behind. Nodding, the grizzled villager hefted his axe and began creeping right, towards the front of the rock formation. Ingram moved left in a wide arc, careful to stay downwind of his target. Soon he spotted Walter across the way, nearly to the mouth of the hollow. Ingram crouched, ready to spring the ambush on Walter's signal. His heart hammered, but his grip on the stake remained rock steady. If their prey lingered unaware, tonight would see an end to at least one servant of evil.

Abruptly the stream of whispers fell silent, replaced by an unnatural stillness. Ingram locked eyes with Walter who gave an almost imperceptible shake of his head. Somehow their quarry sensed the trap was about to spring. A guttural snarl shattered the silence. Then a pale figure burst from the shadows of the rocky hollow, heading straight for Walter's position.

Ingram broke from cover, streaking towards the creature's exposed back. But halfway there, he stumbled to a halt as if striking an invisible wall. The air itself seemed to thicken, resisting his passage. Ingram roared his frustration as the thing that wore the form of a young man closed on Walter, whose axe swept cleanly through the space the creature had just occupied. It moved with demonic speed; pale features twisted with open blood lust.

Fighting the unseen resistance slowing his steps, Ingram struggled to intervene before deadly fangs could find Walter's throat. But deep down, he knew he was too late. Fresh rage flared in his chest, a wrathful fire that would not be quenched until this entire nest of vipers was purged root and stem.

Abruptly the unnatural pressure holding Ingram back seemed to evaporate. In quick strides he closed the distance just as Walter met the demon's frenzied charge. The wickedly sharp axe forced the creature to twist fluidly aside, meeting the weapon's edge with its own unnatural strength. Walter managed a glancing blow to its shoulder that elicited an inhuman shriek. Black lifeblood sprayed the snow as the two figures collided.

Arriving in their midst, Ingram drove his stake deep between the demon's ribs before it could recover. A piercing wail tore the night air. The pale form crumpled at Ingram's feet, flesh shriveling around the carved wood pierced deep in its breast. In moments only a withered corpse remained, a look of agony still etched on its grotesque features.

Ingram spared the pitiful remains only a glance. He clasped Walter's shoulder, searching for any sign of injury. "Are you harmed?"

Walter straightened from where he leaned on his axe haft, shaking his head. "Thanks to you, friend. Your aim was true." He nodded at the blackened husk pierced by the stake. "But I fear your blow has roused the rest against us."

All around, shadowy forms closed in. Red eyes glowed with supernatural malice from the darkness beyond the clearing. A series of whispers echoed strangely between the barren trees as the creatures circled just outside the pale moonlight.

Ingram tensed, Walter at his back. Perhaps the legends were true after all. These demons of darkness could pass unseen and unhindered through night's shroud. And now Ingram and Walter were surrounded with no path left but to fight. So be it.

Gripping his axe, Walter muttered, "Make peace with your gods, lad. This night we sup in their halls."

"Peace," Ingram assured him. "Can only be found at the end of our road. And it does not reside in Odin's corpse-strewn hall." He lifted his head to the uncaring sky.

"Lord, guide our hands this night against your enemies," he prayed. "We fight in your name."

Lifting his stake, Ingram turned to face the glowing red eyes. Let the servants of darkness come. He would teach them to fear the light before this was through.

Chapter Five

A collection of howls echoed between the trees as the vampires circled just outside the pale moonlight. Their unnatural voices overlapped like a swarm of bats fluttering against the edge of hearing. Red eyes flashed with hunger as the pack awaited the first move.

Ingram shifted into a balanced stance, turning slowly to keep the encroaching shapes in view. Beside him, Walter hefted his axe, the sturdy farmer's hands steady despite the terror a rational mind ought to feel when surrounded by such creatures. But Ingram had witnessed the man's unflinching courage before. It seemed a hallmark of the introverted folk who carved out their lives and too-often unmarked graves in this remote valley stalked by ancient evil.

Centering his breathing, Ingram sought that mental stillness he required before battle. Fear was a weapon of the enemy. He must enter a fight calm and focused or panic would open holes in his guard. Emotion would only cloud his instincts in the heat of combat. And against supernatural foes, instinct and reflexes meant the difference between life and blessed oblivion.

Yet baser feelings were difficult to ignore when eyeing demonic forces. Even for Ingram, a veteran of many battles against the infernal, the icy touch of dread still brushed his soul when facing creatures so wholly monstrous. The unnatural timbre of their whispers and coiled, predatory poise inspired primal revulsion. His fists clenched to keep from trembling.

O Lord who guides my hand, grant me clarity to see beyond this veil of fear. Let divine purpose fill my heart, leaving no room for doubt...

Ingram repeated the prayer in his mind until a semblance of calm returned. The vampires had advantages here with their uncanny swiftness and ability to vanish into darkness. But he and Walter retained the upper hand in conviction and courage. The demons cowered from something within their would-be prey. Some spark of grace that seared their light-shunning souls. If Ingram could kindle that holy fire, they would be reduced to cinders in its blaze.

The pack still wavered, wary of making the first move after Ingram's swift destruction of their kindred. But their patience was limited. Hunger gnawed at their unnatural existence, eroding caution. Even now some eyed Walter hungrily, awaiting an exposed flank or moment of distraction.

Ingram's gaze locked with that of a large male haunting the edge of the clearing. Intelligence and calculation lurked in that passing fair face, so like a striking youth but for the infernal hunger in its eyes.

"I know you feel the righteousness emanating from us, demon," Ingram called. "It gives you pause. But your craving for innocent blood outweighs this wise fear, does it not?"

The pack leader's mouth twisted in a mocking smile, displaying the points of his fangs. He returned Ingram's stare boldly, as if divining secrets from Ingram's soul.

"Not fear, hunter," the creature replied, voice melodic but with an unnatural resonance. *"But curiosity. It is long since*

mortals wandered these woods with weapons and open defiance. And never have we encountered crusaders with your...heat."

His unblinking stare burned with intensity. *"The light in your companion shines hot indeed. But yours, Hunter, blazes like the sun itself. What furnace fuels such fire?"* He glided a step closer, pale brow furrowing. *"I must know the taste of it."*

Ingram angled to keep the vampire lord squarely in his field of vision. "The radiance you sense comes not from me, demon, but shines through me. It is the light of God's divine spirit, and its heat shall scour your filth from this world."

He brandished his stake etched with holy symbols. "This relic focuses His cleansing power. Should you taste its kiss, only oblivion awaits."

The pack leader smiled fully, displaying his pointed ivory fangs. *"Your magics hold no terror for me, hunter. But it is no matter..."*

In a burst of extreme speed, he launched straight at Ingram's midsection. Ingram pivoted aside, the creature's nails raking his shoulder as it hurtled past. The vampire lord spun with uncanny skill; lips peeled back in anticipation of hot blood.

But Ingram had continued the motion, ending with his stake already driving up beneath the pale demon's ribs even as it turned. This time the blessed point pierced its heart fully.

Chapter Six

The vampire lord's body convulsed, impaled on the stake. His crimson eyes went wide with shock and agony, bloody tears streaking his once fair face. Black lifeblood welled around the carved wood piercing his unbeating heart. But rather than shriveling to dust as the lesser vampire had, this ancient evil fought to wrench its body free.

Ingram swiftly twisted the stake while muttering prayers of banishment. The writhing demon unleashed an unearthly shriek that echoed between the lifeless trees. Ingram grimaced but held firm, shards of ice needling his ears at the banshee wail.

"May the light of God cleanse you from this world," Ingram intoned through gritted teeth. With a final convulsive jerk, the vampire lord went limp, its ancient body rapidly decomposing around the blessed stake. In moments only a desiccated mummy wrapped in tattered finery lay at Ingram's feet. He swiftly removed the blackened stake before decomposition could taint its sacred blessing.

Walter stood nearby, axe and charms ready, staring at the remains. "The old tales spoke truth. These demons have walked these lands since antiquity." He shook his grizzled head in wonder. "To think such wickedness has festered on my very doorstep all these winters."

Ingram nodded grimly, eyes scanning the surrounding woods. With the pack leader destroyed, its accursed kindred had withdrawn into the shadows. But they were not destroyed, merely leaderless and wary. This battle was far from over.

"Take ease, my friend," he told Walter. "You fought bravely and have seen the power of faith this night. But many of these fiends yet roam free and will continue preying upon your people."

He clasped the farmer's shoulder. "Go now and warn the villagers to fortify themselves. I will continue the hunt alone until the last of these demons is banished from your valley."

Walter hesitated. "You've saved my hide twice over this night. I'll not leave you to face them alone."

Ingram shook his head. "Very well, but your place is with your people. They will need stout hearts like yours before this is through. I will return to the village shortly. Trust in God and tell all who will listen that salvation walks these woods this night."

At last Walter nodded, shoulders bowing under an invisible weight. "I should check on Shannon and the other neighbors. But take care, Hunter. Even leaderless, the pack remains deadly."

Ingram managed a taut smile. "Fear not. I am but an instrument of divine will. There are far worse fates than dying in His service."

With a final searching look, Walter took up his axe and disappeared between the trees, headed back to the threatened village. Ingram watched him depart, envying the simple life of hearth and kin awaiting the stoic farmer. Once he too had dreamed of a peaceful future beyond battling wickedness in the dark. But fate, it seemed, had decreed his road lead ever into shadow.

Turning, Ingram gathered his weapons and blessed charms. Pausing over the vampire lord's withered corpse, he sanctified the ground with holy water so it could not rise again. But he dared not linger. Dawn was a handful of hours away and the remaining pack outside his reach. There was scarce time to eliminate more stragglers this night.

Making his way back to the village, Ingram slipped through the deserted streets like a ghost under the icy moon. No lamps burned behind shuttered windows. Not even watch dogs challenged his stealthy passage. Fear had driven all souls indoors, leaving the lanes barren and stagnant as tombs.

Arriving at the door of the Black Boar inn, Ingram knocked twice but received no response, as expected. The old innkeeper wanted nothing to do with a hunter stalking evil through his village. But the man's fear would not deter Ingram from his righteous task.

Letting himself inside, Ingram secured the door and ascended the creaking stairs. Safe within his cramped chamber, he tended his torn shoulder with holy water, muttering prayers of healing and protection. The slash burned unnaturally but closed under his ministrations. His body would bear many more wounds before this crusade was through.

Though bone-weary, Ingram forced himself to kneel and recite the divine offices as dawn's rosy fingers illuminated the dingy window. The familiar rituals focused his mind on the coming day's preparations. Sleep could wait; it brought only restless dreams haunted by the pleading eyes of those already lost. Better to remain wakeful, planning his next righteous extermination.

When the last prayer echoed into silence, Ingram finally lay down upon the straw bed. But his mind churned on where the remaining vampires might be hiding themselves. They possessed uncanny abilities to vanish into darkness and pass unseen. He suspected their lair must reside somewhere deep beneath the very earth, perhaps in caverns buried beneath the valley's stony bones. But how to find an entrance and ferret them out?

Rest eluded him as the morning hours crept past. Soon the village stirred to life outside. Ingram could wait no longer. Rising, he descended to the common room and called for the reserved innkeeper. The old man emerged reluctantly from the back, suspicion heavy on his craggy features.

"I require an adequate meal before I resume today's work," Ingram informed him. "And knowledge of any cave openings near the forest where dark things might dwell."

The innkeeper's already stern face soured further at this request. He turned toward the fire, muttering under his breath. Ingram's fingers twitched toward his stake, impatience rising. "Do not you villagers realize I fight on your behalf"?

"Mind your elders, pup," the old man growled without turning. "And stick to your proper place. You've stirred up forces best left to slumber."

Ingram exhaled through his nose, calming his temper. Perhaps he should use a different tact.

"Friend, I mean only to help end the evil that has plagued your home," he reasoned. "As innocents continue dying, can any place here be called proper or safe? What knowledge do you have that could help restore light?"

The innkeeper paused; gaze lost in the sputtering flames. Then his narrow shoulders seemed to sag beneath an invisible burden. Still facing the fire, he spoke quietly.

"Aye, you're not wrong. Dark times breed dark deeds." He hesitated, then continued reluctantly. "When I was a lad, we dared each other to go deep into the Widow's Chasm, a cave opening north of town. Queer noises echoed from those depths, and gusts like icy breath would rush out."

He shook his head. "We'd throw stones in till our nerves broke, then flee quick as deer. Never had the courage to explore beyond the entrance." At last, he turned to meet Ingram's gaze. "If devilry dwelled anywhere nearby, I'd wager that cursed hollow."

Ingram clasped the old man's thin shoulder. "My thanks. Your recollection may aid the villages greatly."

Turning to go, he paused at the threshold. "I shall require a pack of supplies for the coming trial. Leave it outside this door."

Without waiting for a reply, Ingram departed. He had a direction now, and precious little daylight to prepare. There was no time to waste on superstitious villagers when an entire nest of vampires awaited extermination. Tonight, God willing, he would take the battle straight to their profane sanctuary.

Chapter Seven

Ingram slipped through the silent village, merging with patches of lingering shadow. A leaden exhaustion weighed upon his limbs, the strain of combat through the icy night finally catching up to his mortal frame. But the rising sun's light invigorated his spirit and mission. This day, God's divine eye turned its merciless gaze upon the valley of darkness. And with its blessed radiance to guide him, Ingram aimed to scour the wickedness from this remote haven.

On the decrepit church's rough-hewn door hung a simple notice: *Closed until the evil departs.* Ingram's jaw tightened. How long had the frightened villagers denied themselves holy refuge and rites? Too long, he vowed. After this night's work, dawn would find the church doors thrown wide once more.

For now, he had preparations to make. Stopping by the tree line, Ingram gathered a bundle of dry kindling and stout branches. He bore them to the overgrown smithy on the village outskirts. There he cleared vines from the stone chimney and lit a small fire with ironworking tools scattered nearby. Soon orange light flickered through cracks in the timber walls as the forge's hearth awoke once more.

Ingram then retrieved his weapons and pack from the inn. The promised supplies consisted only of hard bread, cheese, a small skin of beer, illuminating stones and a lantern. It mattered not. Worldly provisions would play a small role in the coming trial. If God willed it, Ingram would survive on faith alone.

First, he carefully cleaned and blessed his stakes, murmuring prayers over the wood charred by demonic blood. Though he had sanctified many replacements, those stakes carried history. Each notch and stain chronicled a battle won against overwhelming darkness. Their very grain had absorbed the light of God. New stakes required their own proving.

Next, he inspected his garments for damage, making repairs and strengthening the seams. Though he owned little, tending his equipment was a sacrament. Armor, anointed weapons, the humble trappings of his crusade; these allowed him to execute the Lord's will upon the earth. Ingram would not enter the coming battle lacking in any fashion.

Kneeling before the forge, Ingram entered into deep prayer. The endless war waged tirelessly in the shadowed places too often obscured his sacred mission. Surrounded by manifest evil and desperation, maintaining inner light became its own struggle. Only through rigorous introspection could he safeguard the divine spark that fueled his faith and purpose. This vigil watch preserved his spirit.

Hours passed in meditation. A distant bell tolled midday. The dim chapel would be vacant with the priest shut away in his quarters. Ingram rose and departed the silent smithy. Time to send his battered spirit in search of balm.

The church interior was dusty and dank from disuse. Guttering candles cast shadows between neglected pews. At the altar knelt a lone figure in somber robes facing the tabernacle, oblivious to Ingram's quiet approach.

"Bless me father, for I have come to make my confession," Ingram intoned softly.

The priest started, turning with wide eyes. Recognition slowly replaced surprise at seeing the hunter. "Ingram Brown," the father sighed. "I might have known you would appear, stirring trouble in your wake."

Ingram inclined his head. "My troubles are of no import. But I would unburden myself of certain deeds committed under heaven's eye."

The old priest studied him for a long moment, then gestured to the confessional booth. "Very well. Let's examine the spiritual cost of your deeds."

The familiar rite settled Ingram's soul. In the darkened interior, whispered sins and divine forgiveness flowed as countless times before. Gruff advice followed to temper future eagerness with wisdom. Finally, penance given, Ingram emerged feeling renewed through the grace of Christ. This was the true bread of life he required to continue his mission.

Outside the dim chapel, Ingram lifted his face to the stark winter sky. Crimson streaked the peaks where the sun sank low. Night fast approached. Turning towards the waiting dark, Ingram departed to execute heaven's will, untroubled by doubts of his own making. The lonely path ahead held no fear for one who walked in righteous light. Tonight, come what may, his war raged on against the encroaching dark.

Chapter Eight

Twilight softened the harsh contours of the icy landscape as Ingram approached the Widow's Chasm. He had followed the rocky gorge north from the village through gradually rising foothills. Bitter wind wailed between the sheer walls moving ever higher. Somewhere ahead lay the sinister cave mouth where local youths once tested their courage.

Ingram did not share the villagers' superstitions regarding this place. But the unforgiving terrain could easily claim lives, especially at night. Clambering over the boulders lining the ravine bottom, he stayed alert for patches of ice and sudden drops. The fading gloom made the footing increasingly treacherous. Soon he would require the lantern brought from the inn.

Up ahead, the narrow gorge curved sharply before appearing to terminate against a sheer cliff face. Ingram recalled the innkeeper's description of the yawning cave entrance near this dead end. He moved cautiously toward the turn, senses straining. The perfect location for an ambush if any vampires yet roamed free.

At the bend, Ingram doused his lantern and pressed close to the rock wall. Slowly he edged forward until the turn revealed a small open area before the gorge abruptly ended. Dense shadows filled the niche, concealing whatever secrets it held. Ingram held perfectly still, watching those shadows intently for any sign of movement. When several frozen minutes passed with no reaction, he risked a low whistle. The surrounding rocks projected the soft sound up the rock walls. No attack came.

Finally, Ingram extended the dim lantern before him and stepped out. Stones shifted under his boots, echoing off the surrounding cliffs. The flickering light revealed no lurking shapes. But a gaping void marked the cliff where the ravine ended. Approach revealed the mouth of a cavern extending down at a steep angle. The innkeeper's memory had proven accurate. This certainly seemed an ideal lair for creatures seeking refuge from the sun.

With utmost care, Ingram lowered himself over the lip of the cave entrance. Icy stone offered meager handholds as he descended into absolute darkness. The temperature plummeted, his breath coming in ragged plumes. From below echoed the occasional drip of water and skitter of dislodged pebbles. But no other sounds of occupation.

When the grade leveled, Ingram found himself in a low, cramped tunnel barely wide enough to admit his frame. Gripping his strung bow, he edged forward seeking clues any vampires sheltered this deep. But several hundred feet revealed no openings, animal bones or other signs of habitation.

Frustration mounting, he considered turning back. Perhaps this was merely another decrepit cave system, nothing more. But he paused, tilting his head. Was that a murmur of voices from somewhere ahead? Moving as silently as possible, Ingram continued along the claustrophobic tunnel towards the possible sound. If vampires did wander these dark depths, he must locate their nest.

The crude passage narrowed further before opening into a wider chamber. Ingram edged forward until he could peer inside while remaining hidden. Ragged teeth of rock hung from the ceiling, dripping into small pools that echoed strangely. Along the far wall, his lantern revealed a jagged opening that presumably delved deeper still. And from that yawning abyss rose unmistakable echoes of speech in eerie, inhuman tones. Every instinct screamed at Ingram to turn and flee this oppressive darkness teeming with palpable evil. But he forced frozen limbs to comply, moving haltingly towards the sound. His battle lay ahead in the nest of monsters. There could be no retreat now.

Crude stairs had been carved into the stone, spiraling down into unfathomable depths. Ingram descended silently, suppressing an urge to clutch the protective amulets hanging from his belt. The temperature continued dropping until his limbs went numb and even his thoughts slowed. But the murmur of alien voices rose louder, echoing strangely as if from a vast cavern.

The narrow steps ended abruptly, opening into a towering chamber. Ingram hunkered down, peering from the final turn. Beside him yawned a sheer void disappearing into the depths. But across the chamber stood an insane geography of jagged stone that formed ledges and hollows housing unnatural structures. In a great central pit glowed a fitful red light, though its source was obscured.

Squinting against the hellish glare, Ingram glimpsed pale forms lounging or clinging to the stone protrusions like roosting bats. A few sprawled before the fiery pit hidden at the chamber's heart, speaking in voices both hissing and shrill.

Their words meant nothing to him, but a staggered chanting rhythm underlay the discourse. The cadence spoke to primal fears buried in the oldest recesses of Ingram's mind.

This crude sanctuary was utterly profane, but undoubtedly the nest he had been seeking. Surveying the scene, Ingram tallied over a dozen vampires within view, likely only a fraction of those sheltering in this vast cavern. Could he and Walter have triumphed had they breached this abyss together? Ingram murmured a prayer of thanks that he had not led his friend into such unfavorable odds. If these hell spawns were to be destroyed, guile and holy fire must suffice where courage and sharpened wood alone would fail.

With utmost care, Ingram crept back up the icy stairs as quietly as he'd come. This night was not the time to strike. But now he knew the place where the infestation festered. Once back in the village, he could formulate a plan to purify this charnel house with cleansing flames. Until then, vigilance and patience.

The frigid journey back tested Ingram's commitment. More than once his frozen limbs threatened to fail on the treacherous cliffside passage. Fighting through the bone–numbing weariness, Ingram finally emerged into the welcome sting of the night air. Wind scoured his face, reviving numb extremities as he hastened back to the village.

A few lanterns burned behind shuttered windows as Ingram made his way to Walter's cottage. The big man opened his door at Ingram's coded knock, wrinkled face sagging in relief. After securing the door, Walter gripped Ingram's shoulder with a meaty hand.

"Praise the saints, you survived! When others reported screams in the night woods, I feared the hunt had claimed you." His earnest eyes searched Ingram's haunted face. "What evil have you witnessed, my friend?"

Ingram chose his words with care, still piecing together the night's revelations. "The pack has been diminished, but those remaining have retreated deep under the earth. I believe I have located their profane sanctuary." He hesitated. "God willing, it can be collapsed and consecrated. But I cannot accomplish this alone."

Walter's thick brows rose in surprise, but he nodded resolutely. "Just tell me what needs doing. You've carried this burden long enough."

Ingram quickly outlined finding the hidden cave tunnels leading to the vampires' subterranean nest. "We must seal them inside by collapsing the access stairs, then fill the complex with holy fire to purge their evil." He gripped Walter's shoulder. "I would not ask any to shoulder this peril alone. But together, God shall grant us victory."

Walter's eyes kindled with righteous intensity. "A sound plan. I'll gather able men and women on the morrow to begin preparations." He hesitated, searching Ingram's haggard face. "Rest here tonight. You look ready to collapse."

Though Ingram yearned to push on, wisdom prevailed. "Very well, but at first light we begin. Time is against us."

Walter showed him to a small corner chamber before retiring. Ingram secured the threshold with charms and sanctified clay. Kneeling to pray, he wavered as bone–weariness threatened to overtake him. Still, he persisted in completing the divine offices before finally succumbing to sleep. Evil never rested, so nor could he.

Dawn's thin light filtered into Walter's cottage, stirring Ingram from a few fitful hours of sleep. He murmured a prayer of thanks for surviving to see another day, then quickly prepared himself. Dark dreams lurked just beyond memory's edge, awaiting nightfall to resume haunting him. Best to stay busy and focused on their righteous task.

Walter was already outside speaking with a handful of stalwart villagers. Most looked uneasy at openly defying the valley's vampire masters, but Walter's determined conviction seemed to steady their nerves. Ingram also spotted a few faces worthy of suspicion. Likely some had turned secretly or now served the pack against their neighbors. He would need to watch them closely when the time came to collapse the tunnels. But for now, any arm able to swing a pickaxe or haul timbers aided their cause.

As Ingram approached, Walter gripped his shoulder firmly. "Tell them what you told me of the blood drinkers' lair. None before have seen it to tell the tale."

Ingram recounted his exploration under the Widow's Chasm to the gathered villagers. Most stared in frightened awe, making signs against evil at his description of the vampires' subterranean nest. A few men spat oaths, faces clouding with anger as the true depths of the danger facing their kin sank in. One wide-eyed youth looked ready to bolt into the woods.

"This evil has plagued our home too long," Walter declared into the uneasy silence. "But no more! Today we take the first steps to eradicate this scourge from our valley." He brandished a pickaxe and blessed torch. "Who will join the crusade?"

One burly man stepped forward: black eyes hard. "You have my hands, Walter. My wife will rest easier in her grave knowing others are spared her fate." He clasped Walter's shoulder with a meaty hand.

Gradually the other villagers joined in voicing their support, shaking off nervous doubt in the face of Walter's devoted leadership. Soon the group was moving towards the cliffs overlooking the ravine. A new energy invigorated their strides at finally striking back against the shadowy evil haunting generations. Lighting torches and readying equipment, they stood united and purposeful before the abyssal cave mouth. The final battle loomed.

Chapter Nine

Ingram stood at the lip of the cave studying its black depths as the villagers prepared themselves. Fresh gusts hissed from those frigid tunnels, carrying grotesque whispers to tease his ears. The rational mind knew it was only wind disturbing old bones. Yet instinct recoiled from the menace exuding from that abyssal throat. Only faith in their righteous purpose gave him courage to lead the villagers once more into its grasping dark.

Turning to address the group, Ingram beheld their faces glowing with fervent zeal in the torchlight. "Take heart and stand together, friends. God shall grant us victory this day."

They cheered, brandishing pickaxes in challenge to the lurking evil below. Ingram only prayed that their boldness held when confronted by the horrors ahead. But they must strike swiftly before the vampires uncovered this threat to their nest.

"Walter, Miriam, and Thomas, you're with me at the rear," Ingram directed. The level–headed trio nodded grimly. "Phillip, you lead the way with three volunteers. Mark the tunnel walls at fifty paces with these illuminating stones so we do not lose our bearings."

Ingram turned to address the remaining villagers. "The rest follow twenty paces behind Phillip's group. All carry torches high to banish these hellish shadows." Taking a deep breath, he drew his sword etched with holy script. "Let us end the domain of devils this day."

The company cheered again before plunging into the cave mouth. Their mingled torchlight illuminated slick walls glistening with beads of moisture. As the terrain sloped, their breath plumed in the frigid air. A few voices echoed too loudly off the cramped tunnel, eliciting shushes from those behind. But excitement and purpose carried them forward against their primal fears.

Reaching the first turn, Phillip marked the wall with charcoal before continuing the descent. His broad frame led the group steadily through the tight bends and uneven footing. Two hundred paces brought them to a wider section where Ingram first recalled hearing the vampires' eerie voices. He hissed for a halt.

"Beyond this point, make no sound lest we rouse the damned." Nodding their understanding, the line of villagers resumed even more cautiously. Ingram tracked their pace, waiting until the entire group had crawled into the winding tunnel beyond the vampire den's entry chamber.

"Halt and prepare yourselves," he breathed to those around him. "God be with us all."

Pausing to murmur a fervent prayer, Ingram gave the signal. As one, the rear group surged forward, bellowing challenges that echoed ahead. With heavy picks they assailed the walls of the narrow tunnel just before it opened into the larger chamber. Cracks appeared in the ancient stone, dust and debris raining down.

The other groups quickly pushed back through the chaos to aid the effort. More hands lent their strength, widening the cracks splitting the stone. With a great groan, whole sections of the tunnel collapsed, sealing the way behind them in an impassable morass of rubble. But the noise raised an ungodly clamor from the depths as the nest of vampires awoke to attack. All torchlight extinguished at once, plunging the group into absolute darkness.

Ingram swiftly struck flint to tinder, lighting the torch he had prepared. "Stay close and stand your ground!" he shouted, raising the guttering brand against the shadows swarming from the abyss. Glowing eyes converged, accompanied by shrieks that stabbed ice into their veins. Ingram glimpsed writhing pale figures scrabbling over the debris, claws raking the air as they surged mindlessly to attack.

"Hold fast! They cannot reach God's light!" Ingram thrust the torch at the onrushing horde. The creatures recoiled from the wavering flames, pressed against the tunnel sides by their brethren behind. Ingram glimpsed leathery wings unfurling as several vampires prepared to rush over the throng.

"Blessed arrows, loose at will!" he commanded. A volley of shafts streaked overhead, piercing wing membranes and searing cursed flesh. Howls of agony battered their ears, but the creatures continued working to force through the chokepoint tunnel. Their blood-maddened hunger could not be denied.

Ingram knew time was short. "Light your brands and retreat, now!" More torches flickered to life, pushing back the writhing dark. Ingram kept the rear as the group withdrew down the tunnel. Claws grasped just out of range, slamming against his torch when he lingered to fire arrows pointblank into the horde.

Finally reaching the cave mouth, they staggered into blessed daylight and clean air. All gratefully gulped lungfulls of air between ragged cheers. They had delivered a blow, if not yet a mortal one. The celebration kindled needed morale for the next phase ahead.

As Ingram turned to search their faces, he noted one villager slipping quietly away from the group. A broad-shouldered youth who had joined only this morning.

Ingram raced after him, shouting, "Halt, in God's name!" If that traitor made it back to the nest with word, all might be lost. The young man glanced back, eyes widening in fear. Then he began sprinting down the ravine.

With a burst of speed, Ingram launched himself, driving the fugitive to the icy ground. They tumbled and wrestled furiously until Ingram managed to pin his thrashing limbs. The traitor spat and cursed, limbs twitching unnaturally as he sought to escape.

Ingram held him fast. "Tell me true whose side you serve, and I promise salvation!" He pressed his crucifix to the youth's thrashing face. Smoke rose from the sizzling flesh as the sacred icon seared his skin. The thing trapped inside howled in rage and agony.

"Release me, hunter! I serve the crimson lord!" Spittle flew from his peeled-back lips as the demonic spirit writhed under Ingram's grasp. Gradually the unholy energy seemed to bleed away, leaving only a battered and bloodied youth. His eyes rolled wildly in pain and confusion.

Ingram kept the crucifix pressed close. "Who turned you against your kin?" he demanded. "How many more lurk amongst the villagers?"

The traitor sobbed in pain as words tumbled out. *"I know not...lured into the night...woke in darkness to serve or suffer for eternity...*" He clutched at Ingram. *"Please, I did not ask for this curse! End it, I beg you."*

Ingram's features softened with pity. This poor soul had not chosen evil but had been forcefully corrupted. Perhaps his humanity could yet be reclaimed.

"Help me destroy the vampires and you shall find salvation," Ingram vowed, lifting away the crucifix. The youth nodded eagerly. Ingram hauled him to his feet and marched him back to the nervous villagers. He had a plan, but they must move swiftly. There was not a moment to lose.

Chapter Ten

Racing the fading afternoon light, Ingram and a dozen villagers descended to the sealed cave tunnels once more. The traitor, whose earthly name proved to be Simon, led the way, still dazed and unsteady from Ingram's interrogation. But the youth appeared sincere in his wish to turn against the vampires who had corrupted him. Ingram kept a close eye, nonetheless. If their scheme succeeded, Simon would face many more struggles on the path to reclaiming his soul.

Nearing the site of the cave-in, the group halted to ready the materials hauled from the village. Ingram gave quiet instructions as the villagers mixed flasks of sanctified oil and secured rags to torch ends. Once soaked, the brand rags would ignite anything unholy they touched.

"When the battle begins, stay together and remain focused," Ingram urged the nervous villagers. "Our crusade ends today. The monsters we face are vicious but also desperate. Remember that and hold fast."

Taking a lit normal torch, Ingram led the way over the morass of rubble blocking access to the vampire nest. Simon followed, face pale but jaw set. The others lit their holy torches from Ingram's brand and fanned out, prepared to unleash righteous fire. At Ingram's signal, Simon called out in the vampires' fell tongue, pleading for aid.

A chorus of unholy shrieks answered from the abyss beyond the blockage. Thuds and scrabbling sounds rose as the creatures tore at the debris, ripping a passage open. Soon pale limbs slashed through, heedless of torn flesh in their frenzy to reach these intruders. The vampires had taken the bait. Now to spring the trap.

"Ignite and retreat!" Ingram hurled his torch at the nearest vampire whose skin blackened and smoked at the merest touch. Spinning, he fled with the others, holy brands sailing through the air to spread their purifying flames. Howls of agony followed them up the tunnels as the blessed fire found its marks. But not all the vampires were caught in the blaze. As furious hisses sounded behind, Ingram glanced back to see over a dozen monsters bounding in pursuit, eyes aflame.

"Stand your ground!" Ingram commanded. "Together we can defeat them!"

Though they had the advantage of numbers, seeing the onrushing demons paralyzed a few villagers with terror. They turned to flee, only to be pulled down by claws and fangs. Ingram shouldered through to intercept the vampires, stake and blade weaving a deadly pattern. Holy symbols seared cursed flesh, giving the impression of divine protection. But he was still only a man facing monsters. The numbers threatened to overrun his guard.

Just as claws raked towards Ingram's neck, brilliant sunlight speared into the tunnel behind the snarling vampires. They shrieked and cowered from this searing radiance in the eternal gloom of their sanctuary. A deep voice bellowed through the cave as Walter strode into view, holding aloft the sacred spear Ingram had crafted. Sunbeams blazed down its crystalline shaft, banishing the writhing darkness.

"Back to hell with you, demons!" Walter drove the crackling spear through the nearest vampire's chest, collapsing it to dust. The others scattered from his divine wrath, a few bolting back down the tunnel trail. But Walter and Ingram worked in tandem with the remaining loyal villagers to corner and destroy the last of the disoriented beasts. Soon only smoldering ash and echoing screams sounded in the tunnels.

As survivors sagged in exhaustion, Ingram gripped Walter's arm. "Your timing was most fortuitous, my friend. I feared this crusade had reached its end."

Walter grasped his shoulder. "You led them into the very den of evil. I could do no less." He held up the beaming spear. "This relic turned aside the devil's servants as you promised."

Ingram managed a tired smile. "All thanks to God, not I." He turned to the surviving villagers. "But come, our victory remains incomplete while their cursed nest remains intact. We must——"

A terrific concussion shook the tunnel, cutting him off. All staggered to keep their feet as debris rained down. A great roaring rush followed, like a flash flood through a narrow canyon. Then an explosive burst of scorching air from below, carrying cinders and a reek of brimstone.

"The entire warren is aflame!" Ingram bellowed over the tumult. "Flee for your lives! God, grant we brought enough righteous fire!"

Turning, he drove the group ahead through the quaking tunnels. The aged stone groaned alarmingly, cracks splitting overhead to drip freezing water. They scrambled desperately over piles of loose rubble and around huge boulders shaken loose from above. A hellish glow flickered into view up ahead.

"Do not look back, only ahead to the light of day!" Ingram knew their only hope was to outrun the purifying inferno consuming the ancient vampire nest. If they faltered or lost hope, all would be lost. He shouted fervent prayers, herding the last stragglers ahead by sheer force of will until clean air broke over them.

Collapsing on the icy slope outside, they turned to stare wide-eyed down into the abyss. A great rushing roar continued to build until suddenly a gout of flame burst through the cave mouth. Bright as the sun it seared the sky, sending a tangible shock wave over the land. The entire mountain face trembled, sagging inward over the hidden tunnels far below.

Then slowly, almost gently, the ancient stone began collapsing in on itself. The gaping cave mouth disappeared into a sinkhole spewing flames and debris. Fresh cracks shot rapidly as lightning up the cliffside as tens of thousands of tons of rock shifted and fell ponderously inward. The villagers clapped hands to ears against an awful rending rumble as the vampire nest imploded, consumed by righteous fire.

Finally, the quaking stilled. Where the cave entrance had been, now gaped a sheer crater screened by roiling smoke and dust. The villagers stared in numb disbelief that this smoldering void was all that remained of the ageless evil that had tormented their home. Then cheering broke out, the sound carrying down the valley echoing from its guardian peaks. They had won.

Ingram closed his eyes, adding his own prayer of thanks to their joyous relief. This valley and its people were free at last from the pall of darkness. Now cleansing light could pour over the land, banishing shadows where monsters once lurked. Their tribulations were ended.

As weary villagers clapped Ingram's shoulder in heartfelt gratitude, his gaze fell upon Simon, the youth they had freed from the vampire's curse. But rather than celebrating, the boy stared at the burning pit with a look of profound loss. Ingram's brow furrowed in concern. Though the evil's physical hold was broken, deep wounds remained upon Simon's tortured soul. Their true victory would be reclaiming him fully, as well as this valley, for the realm of light.

Leaving the villagers to savor their triumph, Ingram approached the forlorn youth and spoke gently. "Take heart, Simon. You are delivered from evil's grasp. Now begins the journey back into God's grace. I shall aid you however I'm able."

Simon turned slowly, eyes glistening with remorse and hope. "Do you promise, hunter?" His voice caught roughly in his throat, as though unaccustomed to speaking from the heart. "I wish only to be made clean again."

Ingram gripped his shoulder. "By God's grace, you shall."

Together they turned and descended the winding trail as the last flames guttered out over the vampires' grave. A new era dawned in this remote haven, and Ingram's work here had only just begun.

Chapter Eleven

Ingram stood atop a craggy outcrop, surveying the remote valley now cleansed of evil. Golden light slanted between snow-capped peaks to bathe the rugged landscape. The air felt tangibly changed, as if a crushing weight had lifted to allow easy breaths for the first time in memory. In the village below, lamps glowed in windows while smoke rose cheerily from chimneys. Even from this distance, Ingram sensed the rejuvenating spirit of celebration and hope.

The sound of labored footsteps announced Walter's approach. Ingram turned with a weary smile as the broad-shouldered farmer joined him on the windswept overlook. Walter blew out an explosive breath, hands braced on his knees.

"Whew...this thin mountain air still troubles me," Walter wheezed. "But 'tis a wondrous view."

Ingram nodded. "It heartens me to see life flourishing in the valley again."

Walter's weathered face crinkled around a smile. "All thanks to you, my friend. Our valley will never forget what you've done." He gripped Ingram's arm. "Come, walk with me. Folks are gathering in the village square."

They set off along the scenic mountain path, companionably quiet. A hawk's piercing cry echoed overhead. As the trail wound down through fragrant evergreens, evidence of the vampires' defeat gradually emerged.

Arriving in the village, Ingram took in the changes since that first night he slipped in like a thief. Passing the aged chapel, Ingram was heartened to see the doors propped open. Villagers had already swept the stone floors clear of dust and relit the votives. Tonight, the local priest would lead a cleansing ritual to consecrate the altar and images anew. Another step in reclaiming holy ground from the vampires' desecration.

Windows now stood open, letting in fresh air and golden light. Wreaths of wildflowers and herbs decorated thresholds, replacing the vampires' hated garlic. The scent of woodsmoke and roasting meat filled the lanes where once only fear and despair lingered. Everywhere villagers exchanged joyful greetings, faces alight with renewed faith.

In the village square, trestle tables practically bowed under platters of hard bread, roasted fowl, and stewed vegetables. Ale skins sloshed as men laughed and joked, faces rosy with friendliness. Children darted underfoot, squealing joyfully. The haunted tension that had gripped every soul mere days before now seemed but a fading nightmare.

"It heartens me to see our home coming back to life," Shannon said after a comfortable silence. "Laughter lifts the spirit like nothing else can. For the first time I feel we're truly delivered from evil."

Walter led the way to a table of honor at the head of the gathering. There the village leaders rose to clasp Ingram's hand, faces framing weary smiles that only recently learned happiness again. As Walter made introductions, one elder gripped Ingram's shoulder with gnarled hands.

"Young master, we owe you more than these poor words can repay," he rasped, rheumy eyes bright with feeling. "Ask anything of us, and consider it done."

Ingram ducked his head. "I need no reward beyond seeing health and cheer restored here."

"Nevertheless, you shall have it," the elder insisted. "Your arrival seemed heaven-sent, and we are not mistaken in that, nor ungrateful."

Seeing argument would not deter their wishes, Ingram simply bowed acceptance. He took a seat of honor as mugs of ale were raised in frequent toasts to his deeds. Platters came heavy with roasted game, fresh baked bread, and stewed roots harvested from newly blessed fields. Together the village celebrated their liberation from darkness.

Deeply moved, Ingram clasped Walter's broad shoulder. "There is no need for thanks between friends. Only the work ahead, healing wounds so we might walk together in the light."

Walter smiled and lifted his mug in salute. "Well said!" More cheers rang out as he turned and called for the feast to continue. Soon merriment once more flowed freely as platters were passed and songs raised in celebration of their deliverance.

Ingram partook sparingly, smiles not quite reaching his eyes. A bone-deep exhaustion permeated his spirit, so he ate very little. He was unused to such lightness after inhabiting the valley's darkness for so long.

Glancing around at the joyful throng, he felt a pang of detachment. He did not fully belong in their sunlit world anymore. Though he still felt removed from the boisterous crowd, their joyous spirit lightened his heart enough to share quiet laughter with newfound friends.

For this precious interlude, he would set down his mantle of duty and darkness. Tonight, even his scarred soul might know a few hours of light and refuge.

As the feast wound down and relatives led drowsy children home, Walter suggested a stroll. "There's something I would show you," he said. Ingram bade their hosts goodnight and followed Walter down quiet lanes beneath the glimmering mountain sky. They passed Walter's snug cottage and adjacent barn, entering a wide pasture at the valley's edge. There Walter approached a stone cairn topped by a simple wooden cross. Kneeling, he passed a broad hand over the mound.

"Here lie the bones of my ancestors, who carved a life from this rock and soil," Walter murmured. He was silent for a long moment before continuing. "My father rests here. The vampires took my mother. He had to..." Walter's deep voice grew hoarse. "So, she would not rise as one of them."

Ingram placed a gentle hand on his stooped shoulder. "There is no shame in freeing loved ones from such a fate."

Walter swallowed hard. "We never told my sisters how she died. Only that the monsters took her as they did so many others." He looked up at Ingram, eyes shining in the dimness. "But no more. You brought us deliverance."

"Through God's grace," Ingram amended. "I merely helped strike the blow."

Rising, Walter gripped his shoulder with a heavy hand. "A prophet's humility does you credit, my friend. But make no mistake, you are this valley's savior." His stern face relaxed into an unfamiliar smile. "Come, there is more I would show you."

Walter led the way to a farmhouse apart from the rest, lamplight glowing invitingly from its windows. As they entered the cozy home, rich cooking smells enveloped them. Shannon appeared from the back room, face lighting up at the sight of Ingram.

"You're just in time," she welcomed them. "I've prepared a special meal in thanks."

Despite Ingram's mild protests, she soon had him seated at the humble table with a small feast spread before him. Walter occupied himself stoking the hearth fire while Shannon bustled about, refilling emptied platters and mugs. Her injured leg still held a slight limp, but seeing her alive and well untied the knot guilt had left in Ingram's chest.

At last full to bursting, the two men retired to the parlor while Shannon tidied up. Walter soon nodded off in a comfortable chair, exhausted by a day of hard labor and revelry.

Alone with his thoughts, Ingram found his mind wandering back to past battles that ended less joyously than this one. Dark memories crowded close, seeking to smother the flickering hope lit within him these past days. With an effort, he banished the shadows, murmuring prayers of thanks and healing. God grant that warm light would continue spreading through this valley, melting away the last remnants of dread and sorrow.

The stairs creaked softly as Shannon descended, carrying a woolen blanket. With a tender smile, she tucked it around the sleeping Walter, whose snoring continued uninterrupted. Then she joined Ingram on the hearth stones, hands wrapped around a steaming mug.

"Your burdens remain heavy, though you carry ours no more. It heartens me to see our home coming back to life," Shannon said after a comfortable silence. "Laughter lifts the spirit like nothing else can. For the first time I feel we're truly delivered from evil."

Ingram nodded, the dancing flames chasing the shadows away. He turned to see Shannon regarding him somberly. The lass looked wan but spirited, the haunted shadows retreating from her eyes.

He managed a weary smile. "We all bear wounds from the trials endured. But let this be a day for you to celebrate life's brightness, not linger on grim thoughts."

Shannon's expression turned sympathetic. "And for you? When shall be your day to rejoice and give thanks?"

Ingram looked away, throat tightening. Since walking this lonely path, solace rarely touched his spirit. He lived immersed in a shadow world far removed from simple pleasures. Yet glimpsing such joy kindled an ember of longing even his stoic heart could not deny.

Gently Shannon took his hand in hers. "Stay a while, friend. Allow our hearts to warm you." She searched his downcast eyes, her own shining earnestly. "The darkness will wait, but moments like these are precious and fleeting. Will you not linger to share our joy?"

Her words pierced Ingram's guard, unleashing a well of pain and weariness. He shut his eyes, swaying slightly. Shannon quickly braced him as hot tears slipped free, years of trauma finally breaching his fortified soul.

Gradually the flood passed, leaving Ingram hollowed out but cleansed. Raising reddened eyes, he found no judgment on her face, only compassion. Swallowing past a thick lump in his throat, Ingram rasped humbly, "Forgive me, I don't know what came over me..."

Shannon shushed him gently. "There is naught to forgive, dear friend. Your tears proclaim your humanity, not weakness." She smiled through her own glistening eyes. "Will you accept our companionship a little longer? Let these valleys provide a sanctuary for us all to heal?"

Ingram drew a shuddering breath, then nodded slowly. Perhaps lingering in this haven a few days would allow him to mend and fortify his spirit for the road ahead. And for the first time since embarking on this lonely crusade, a sense of peace softened his guard. Here were true helpmeets to walk with him awhile, sharing earnest care untainted by fear or despair.

Chapter Twelve

Over the following weeks, life in the remote village attained an idyllic rhythm free of the pall of dread. Clearing winter skies brought thaws that opened paths and allowed eager hands to repair damage left by the vampire occupation. Crumbled sections of wall and roof emerged patched sturdier than before. Fresh whitewash concealed lingering scorch marks from holy fire. The derelict chapel was consecrated anew after a solemn funeral for those lost in the final crusade.

Throughout these hopeful changes, Ingram lingered but remained apart. He busied himself creating charms and balms to aid the healing. But his restless spirit chafed at this pastoral pace, like a caged hawk longing to stretch its wings again. Peaceful pursuits could not fulfill someone so long immersed in shadows. Yet neither could he bring himself to depart the first place that had felt like a home in too long. For now, he lingered in limbo, struggling to reorient his path.

Late one morning found Ingram carefully harvesting elder branches along a sun–dappled trail. A hermit thrush trilled overhead as if approving his gentle care for the living wood. As he sliced the pith to craft flutes for local children, his thoughts drifted to the road ahead. Reports told of a remote abbey plagued by a dark presence stalking their forest sanctum. Ingram's skills would be welcomed there.

But furtive threats seemed pale compared to the towering evil recently defeated here. What sacred duty compelled him to abandon this haven for the unknown perils beyond? Sighing, Ingram slipped his whittling knife back into his coat. How could one be certain when signs pointed different ways?

Hoofbeats broke his introspection. Simon trotted into view, astride a rangy roan mare pulling a cart with supplies from a distant valley settlement. The youth looked transformed from the haunted creature lately freed from the vampires' curse. His cheeks had lost their pallor, and bright purpose now filled his eyes. At Ingram's smile, Simon swung down gracefully.

"Well met, my friend. I hope your journey proved uneventful?" Ingram began helping unload grain sacks and tools from the cart.

"Right peaceful, it was," Simon assured. "These valleys feel changed now, as if a dark fog has lifted to reveal the sun again. Folk are stirring from their homes ready to rebuild." His smile faltered briefly. "Some offer thanks to me for my small part. I know not how to accept it."

Ingram clasped his shoulder. "Take their words as balm, not praise," he advised gently. "Their gratitude helps heal wounds we all share." Simon nodded, appearing buoyed.

Together they distributed the supplies, saving parcels for Walter, Shannon and other villagers who had shown Ingram kindness. His ever–busy thoughts quieted during these basic tasks. It seemed that helping others might impart the direction he craved. If one walked with faith, the correct path would emerge in time.

Weary but satisfied, they paused outside Walter's cottage as sunset gilded the valley. Raucous laughter carried from inside where the household was likely gathered for their evening meal. Ingram felt torn between intruding and heading back to his lonely room at the inn. Sensing his indecision, Simon gave a kindly smile.

"Come, let us feast with my uncle," the youth urged. "His family always sets two extra places, one of which is surely meant for you." Taking Ingram's arm, he led the way inside the cheery warmth of hearth and lamp.

Young faces brightened around the worn table before Walter's stentorian voice declared, "Here are the heroes of the hour!" Ingram found himself heartily clasped and ushered to the head of the board. Soon steaming bowls were passed and comfortable conversation flowed, easing the ache of solitude Ingram usually carried. Lingering ghosts seemed to recede from the room's amity.

Later, as the little ones nodded off before the fire, Walter drew Ingram and Simon aside. "While you were away, I received an odd missive," he rumbled, frowning at the logbook where he recorded village matters. "A monk asking after you, Ingram."

He glanced up. "Seemed to think our valley some den of sin that you were charged with purging. I informed him the only purging was of an evil far darker than he realized. A naïve soul, I'd wager, sealed away behind abbey walls. But I thought you should know in case this hermit seeks you out with more letters or mission orders."

Ingram nodded thoughtfully. Perhaps this monk was a herald of the very mission Ingram had contemplated earlier that day. It seemed providence if he believed in such things.

Simon leaned forward eagerly. "Does this mean you'll be moving on from our valley soon?" His high spirits dimmed somewhat at the prospect.

Slowly Ingram nodded. "I cannot remain indefinitely now the crusade here has ended. There are always other villages plagued by shadow. My duty is to bring them light."

"Then I shall go with you!" Simon exclaimed. "You'll need a loyal companion on the road." His youthful features set in firm lines.

Ingram considered the offer, touched by his spirit but uncertain it was a wise path. "You have a place here, Simon, and a family that needs you." He gestured around Walter's cottage, ablaze with love and life.

Undeterred, Simon met his eyes staunchly. "Because of you, I have my soul back and a future unshackled from evil. I would use my life in service to our shared cause." His gaze pleaded for understanding. "Please, allow me to fight at your side."

Moved by his devotion, Ingram clasped Simon's shoulder. "If you insist, I would be honored by your companionship. We shall strike out together as soon as I settle affairs here." Simon grinned, wringing his hand eagerly. Sometimes youth's passion outshone wisdom, but perhaps this crusade would need his energy.

Walter looked bemused if unsurprised by this development. "Cannot say I relish my last living kin venturing into danger," he admitted. "But the boy has steel in him, thanks to you. I suppose the solace of nature and home may always elude those called to a higher road." He embraced Simon roughly. "Do what honor decrees, lad. This valley will keep a light burning to guide your way home."

They spoke long into the night about preparations for the journey ahead. When Ingram finally departed for the inn, an unfamiliar sense of purpose filled his steps. For the first time in long years, he had a destination beyond chasing phantoms in the dark. A mission was crystallizing through the valley's extended peace.

Perhaps his time here had served a divine purpose beyond vanquishing vampires. Watching Simon transform had rekindled Ingram's own passion for this vital work. He would take inspiration from the light of this haven and its people as he ventured forth. Wherever the forces of corruption arose, Ingram now knew he and Simon would answer humanity's call.

Chapter Thirteen

Ingram stood upon a ridge overlooking the remote valley, taking in its craggy peaks limned with dawn's rosy light. Birdsong echoed through the pristine air, unmarred by any sound of strife. It was the idyllic haven he had glimpsed that first night from its shadowed boundary. Thanks to the efforts of many, innocence and beauty now thrived here unfettered.

Hoofbeats heralded Simon's approach upon his sturdy mare. Spying Ingram, his face lit with a ready smile. "Ready to depart this paradise, my friend? I confess I shall miss its tranquil charms and mother's cooking."

Ingram nodded, breathing deep the crisp air. "I too shall yearn for this place. Few locations have offered such fellowship and peace." He held Simon's shoulder. "But the wider world awaits, in need of the strength we have forged here."

Turning their backs on the valley, they set off along the winding trail. When they crested the final ridge, Ingram reined his horse and paused to look back. There in the distance stood Walter and Shannon, raising their hands in farewell. Ingram lifted an arm in return salute, emotions swelling his chest. Then he faced forward and set off without glancing back again. That blessed refuge would stay graven on his heart, seeding future days of darkness with hope.

Simon set an eager pace as they descended the rugged foothills. "How far to this abbey?" he queried. "I am ready to confront whatever evil next crosses our path."

Ingram smiled at his enthusiasm. "Patience, my friend. Our road promises many trials to test courage and faith." He pointed towards a hazy blue ridgeline peeking above the distant trees. "Our destination lies across those peaks. We should arrive before nightfall on the third day, God willing."

"Is it true demonic forces have stained the abbey's sanctity?" Simon asked, devouring the trail ahead with his eyes. "The monk's letter seemed vague on details."

"I know only rumors passed from villages on the abbey's fringe," Ingram said. "Some malefic presence dwells in the forest, targeting holy brothers during their woodland devotions. Several have disappeared over the past year." He scanned the surrounding trees warily. "The survivors speak of a dark spirit that drives men to madness or renders them incapable of describing the evil."

Simon made the sign against wickedness. "It sounds dire as the vampire menace once plagued our valley. What do you suspect awaits us there?"

Ingram opened his mouth to respond when a prickle on his neck cut him short. Reining up sharply, he held up a forestalling hand. The birdsong and insect chatter of moments before had ceased abruptly. An unsettling pall hung over the shaded trail and surrounding trees. Simon froze, eyes alert as his hand crept toward the sword at his hip.

Slowly Ingram turned in the saddle, nostrils flaring to catch any whiff of corruption on the still air. But nothing seemed amiss among the dappled shadows. Cursing his nerves, Ingram shook off the sensation. Perhaps the valley's peace had dulled his battle instincts.

"My apologies," he muttered. "Thought I sensed..." Trailing off, Ingram nudged his horse forward again. "No matter. We should reach the next village by dusk."

Simon peered a moment longer into the dense trees before trotting after. "I thought I felt something strange as well," he admitted. "An...absence...as if a void lurked where the forest's vitality should reside." He shivered slightly. "But I suppose aged woods carry some lingering darkness, like a scar on the land."

Ingram nodded, fighting an irrational desire to spur his horse into a gallop. "Well said. Ancient places acquire some pall of sorrow. It is only reverent to acknowledge that shadow which time cannot erase."

Tossing aside his unease, he kept the conversation light as they traversed slopes gradually rising towards the distant mountains. The forest took on an open, wholesome aspect again. Birdsong resumed overhead, easing their disquiet. Ingram allowed no more distraction from reaching their destination and discovering what evil had tainted its sanctity. Any other diversions would be left for the road ahead.

Chapter Fourteen

The nondescript village nestled in a modest valley between the rising foothills came into view as the afternoon waned towards dusk. Wood smoke scented the air above humble thatched roofs ragged from a long winter. Chickens scattered across the main track at their approach. A mangy hound bayed halfheartedly before slinking off into the gloom between buildings.

Ingram was unconcerned with the poverty evident around them. His travels had taken him through countless desperate hamlets and forgotten wanderers' camps. Wherever darkness flourished, human dignity and spirit suffered. These faces showed wariness, but not the stark fear he had witnessed under the vampires' occupation. Here was but one village among thousands needing light.

Near the muddy town square, an inn's crooked placard proclaimed vacancies in faded letters. Ingram directed their horses towards its stable yard with relief. "We'll secure lodging for the night."

Simon glanced sidelong at him. "And a meal more appealing than my trail rations, I hope."

Ingram huffed a laugh. "Yes, we have earned some modest comforts after the day's long ride. Even warriors cannot live on prayer and resolution alone."

He tried not to think of Walter's convivial table, always graced with savory stew. Such pleasant nostalgia would only feed regret over departing that sanctuary. Ingram could not dwell on what lay behind or vainly desire comfort. The stark days ahead promised little ease.

Entering the dim, low-ceilinged inn, Ingram rang the bell on the bar to summon the keeper.

The innkeeper shuffled out, rag in hand and eyes suspicious. But upon seeing two travel-worn yet decently attired wayfarers, his demeanor warmed slightly.

"A room for the night and stabling for our horses," Ingram requested, placing a few silver coins on the scarred bar. "And whatever provisions your kitchens can furnish for supper."

The man swept the coins into his apron and nodded. "Aye, we've space enough. I'll have the boy tend your mounts." He squinted at Ingram more closely. "You've the look of a cleric. We don't get many men of faith in these parts."

Ingram exchanged a glance with Simon. "We journey to the abbey in the northern ranges," he explained carefully. "I am counted as a friend by the brothers there."

The innkeeper crossed himself. "Queer tidings from those parts lately. Brother Lucas passed through not long ago, bound there on some urgent mission. An intense fellow, scarred of face." He lowered his voice. "I'd steer clear of that place if I were you. Godly souls have met dark ends in its shadowed halls."

Simon leaned forward eagerly, but Ingram forestalled him with a look. "Truly? We had heard disturbing rumors and mean to discern their validity." He passed another coin across the bar. "What else did this Brother Lucas share before heading into peril?"

The innkeeper pocketed the money. "Spoke of the tainted forest and missing monks. And an ancient evil regaining strength on Samhain's night." He shook his grizzled head. "Don't meddle with those black arts, I say. Brother Lucas had witchcraft in his eye. He'll come to no good end."

Ingram absorbed this unsettling news. Samhain, the pagan new year, was but a fortnight away. If some profane ritual was slated to occur, their timing could not be worse. He needed to discover more about this mysterious Lucas's intentions.

"We shall heed your counsel, friend," Ingram assured the worried innkeeper. "Our journey is merely to provide spiritual comfort to the remaining brothers." He gestured to Simon. "My apprentice here has some skill in scribing, so we may compile an illuminated manuscript for their refuge."

The innkeeper nodded, features softening slightly. "A worthy goal. Just mind you keep to holy tasks, not chasing evil best left alone." He shuffled back towards the kitchen. "I'll have the boy bring up a meat pie soon as it's warm."

Ingram led Simon upstairs to a cramped but clean room beneath the eaves. Once the door was secured, Simon turned eagerly. "This is providence! Not only are we anticipated, but we know precisely when the danger will manifest." His grin faltered at Ingram's stern expression.

"This complicates matters," Ingram said grimly. "I mislike meddling with powers linked to pagan rites we barely comprehend. And this Brother Lucas sounds an erratic ally if indeed his goals align with ours." He shook his head. "I must spend tonight in vigil and prayer to seek answers."

Chastened, Simon nodded agreement. But as they conversed over a humble dinner of meat pie and ale downstairs, Ingram saw the lad's appetite for action had not lessened. Youth ever rushed toward peril, seeing only opportunity for great deeds. Ingram must temper this recklessness with wisdom and ensure they approached the abbey prepared in both body and spirit. The purest courage still required divine guidance when confronting ancient evil.

After securing their room, Ingram and Simon descended to the common room. Ingram had hoped for a quiet corner to begin his meditations, but raucous music filled the low-beamed space. A red-faced fiddler sawed energetically in one corner while the crowd clapped along or partnered up for energetic reels that shook the floorboards.

Realizing prayer would be impossible, Ingram gestured to Simon. "Perhaps you should join the festivities. I will take some air by the stables."

Simon's face lit up. "A fine idea! My limbs grow stiff from long days ahorse." Casting his cloak aside, he eagerly pushed into the boisterous throng, soon whirling some local maid with infectious enthusiasm.

Ingram slipped outside to the quiet of the damp stable yard. Finding a dry barrel in an open shed, he settled atop it and tilted his head back to observe the emerging stars. The inn's noise faded to a distant thrumming as his mind emptied, letting the vast beauty of the cosmos replace mundane thoughts. Nature's purity could cleanse spirits overburdened by tragedy or malice. He sought that inner quiet to better understand the meaning in events unfolding around them.

Gradually Ingram noticed a discordant energy disrupting the peaceful night. The horses in nearby stalls shifted restlessly, their soft whinnies and hoof stomps carrying a note of distress. Ingram's pulse quickened as he scanned the inky shadows around the yard.

A pale mist gathered in the open stable doorway, coalescing into the faint shape of a cowled figure that hovered at the threshold. Chill air kissed Ingram's cheek as a ghostly voice echoed from beneath the wraith's hood.

"You travel the road to Raven's roost...heed the crosswind's warning, which carries those taken..."

Ingram rose swiftly, his hand moving to the charms at his belt. But the phantasmal shape dissipated before he could challenge its presence. The uneasy horses quieted, leaving only the faint music and laughter from the inn.

Unease skittered along Ingram's spine. Had a trapped soul sought him out to share insight or a threat? The Crossroads were perilous this time of year when the veil grew thin. Whatever its origin, the eerie warning could prove helpful or dangerous.

Ingram had drawn his chalks to scribe the wraith's message beneath the wagon shed when approaching voices made him swiftly pocket the runes. Two staggering figures entered the stable yard, carrying a small keg between them. Their drunken argument halted abruptly at the sight of Ingram.

"Here now, this be private property," the larger one slurred indignantly, squinting at Ingram. His companion hiccupped, struggling to remain upright.

Ingram moved carefully away. "Apologies, friends. I was just... stepping outside." He edged around the pair, not wanting trouble.

"Not s'fast," the first man challenged, swaying into his path. "Y'have the look of a meddler, sneakin' round where ya shouldn't." He elbowed his companion roughly. "Right, Eamon?"

The smaller man blinked owlishly. "Suppose so."

Before Ingram could respond, the brute threw a wild, lumbering punch. Ingram sidestepped the blow, catching the man's wrist and using his momentum to send him sprawling face–first in the mud. The oafish Eamon barely tried to put up his fists before Ingram landed a sharp kick to his backside that dropped him beside his groaning partner.

Brushing dirt from his hands, Ingram briefly considered teaching them a harsher lesson. But drink caused as much trouble as demons in most villages. He settled for fetching the constable to pour them into a cell to sleep it off.

Returning to the now–quiet common room, Ingram found Simon sipping ale alone by the hearth. The lad grinned when Ingram recounted the scuffle, eyes gleaming with excitement. "We make quite the righteous pair already! Word will spread, and evil shall quake wherever we tread."

Ingram smiled at his intensity. "Let us not seek glory before our work begins. Though I admit a bit of fisticuffs helps unwind the spirit." He nodded to the stairs. "Come. We have many leagues yet ahead and should rest while we can."

Ingram slept fitfully, troubled by formless dreams where a ghostly voice chanted familiar names now lost to his memory. But the pale morning light banished the uneasy night visions. Today they would reach the abbey and begin discovering what evil had tainted its halls. Ingram said fervent prayers for guidance and discernment. If Satan's malice truly awaited them, they must stand fast in the armor of God.

After a simple breakfast, Ingram made discreet inquiries about Brother Lucas but found no fresh details. Donning his cloak and weapons, Ingram strode purposefully into the chill dawn. On this day their true quest began. Whatever secrets the abbey held, he placed his faith in a just Providence to guide their steps.

The faded lavender sky heralded dawn as Ingram and Simon departed the ramshackle village. Frost limned the grass alongside the rutted track, crunching under their horses' hooves. Ingram inhaled the bracing air, exhaling puffs of vapor. The cold clarity lent focus to his thrumming determination. Today their quest began in earnest.

Topping a rise, the abbey came into view nestled in a remote valley. Gray stone walls enclosed cultivated plots fading to untamed forest beyond. Tendrils of mist clung to wild meadows surrounding the sanctuary, as if seeking to reclaim that civilized oasis. Faint tolls echoed from the bell tower, summoning the faithfully devout. To Ingram, they sounded a clarion call to action.

Simon shifted eagerly in his saddle. "At last, our journey finds purpose! I pray the monks have insights on vanquishing this evil."

"And that it does not vanquish them first," Ingram muttered, brow creased as he searched for signs of corruption marring the tranquility below. But nothing yet betrayed the lurking threat hinted at in frightened whispers and faded letters.

Descending the winding trail, buildings took shape through the swirling mists. Stern fortifications surrounded ornamental cloisters and arched windows hinting at refinement within. Chad robed figures crossed between edifices on quiet errands. The aura of piety and dedication emanating from this bastion heartened Ingram. Surely grace abounded enough to withstand the encroaching darkness.

They passed through the gatehouse unchallenged, heading toward the chapel nestled against soaring ramparts. But the mournful toll of bells stayed their steps. Approaching slowly, they witnessed a humble funeral procession, bearing a shrouded form on a wooden bier. The cowled participants sang dirges, censers wafting pungent incense.

Ingram made the blessing sign, murmuring, "May flights of angels carry thee to thy rest." The abbey had already suffered losses. They must unravel this mystery swiftly before more innocents fell prey.

Monks bearing the bier disappeared through the cemetery's wrought iron gates. Others scattered to their tasks, leaving the curving path empty save for a sharp–faced man in robes hurrying along clutching documents. His cassock bore strange symbols unfamiliar to Ingram, and his tonsured pate gleamed with some ancient marking only visible when caught by the rising sun.

The monk slowed, eyes narrowing when he spied the two unfamiliar men. His penetrating gaze lingered on Ingram, seeming to divine his innermost secrets. Ingram stood calmly under the scrutiny.

"You must be Brother Lucas," he ventured. "The village innkeeper described you on the road here. Well met."

Brother Lucas drew himself erect, unnatural fire burning in his deep–set eyes. His gaze bored into Ingram as if trying to peel away layers to glimpse what lay beneath.

"The innkeeper has a loose tongue," the monk said sharply. "But too much drink addles his mind, I deem." His piercing look turned on Simon. "You travel in curious company, boy."

Before Simon could bristle at being called boy, Ingram stepped forward placatingly. "I am Ingram of Gault, and this is my squire, Simon." He paused. "We understand you have urgent business at the abbey. Might we offer assistance?"

The monk's severe features remained wary. "What brings armed men unbidden to our sanctuary on the eve of the old rites?" His eyes narrowed. "I smell witchcraft upon you. Have you come to consort with those forces set to rise?"

Ingram shook his head firmly. "On my honor, we aim only to combat the evil you have suffered. Unless all good folk unite against it, darkness may claim these lands completely."

Brother Lucas studied his open face, seeming to weigh his words. Finally, he beckoned them to walk with him.

"Desperate times make for strange allies," the monk muttered as they moved through the compound. "If you speak true, then your mettle shall shortly be tested."

He led them to a nondescript door near the refectory. Glancing about, Lucas produced an iron key that opened the way to a narrow staircase descending into musty darkness. Their footsteps echoed oddly in the steep confines until the overhead light faded completely. Ingram muttered a soft prayer in the oppressive blackness.

At the base awaited a heavy oak door reinforced with iron bands. Lucas traced an intricate glyph on its surface before pulling it open with a groan of stiff hinges. Lifting the torch he had kindled, he led them inside a windowless chamber. Crude writing covered the stone walls from floor to ceiling.

"This crypt holds all the abbey's arcane knowledge," Lucas intoned, lifting the torch high. "Each abbot adds hard-won secrets gleaned battling pagan forces." He turned to face them, eyes burning in the torchlight. "Now you have seen what few alive ever have. Will you join our crusade to banish the darkness rising?"

Ingram's pulse quickened at the prospect. "You have my vow and whatever strength God grants me in this righteous task."

Simon thumped his chest. "Mine as well! We already helped purge a valley overrun by hell spawn."

Lucas nodded solemnly. "Good. Then heed my words well." Beckoning them closer to the walls, he began reading:

"In eras past, the veil between the pagan cosmos and ours grew thin as Samhain approached, allowing eldritch forces to slip through." He traced a line etched deeply into the stone. "The ancient druids learned to harness this power with blood rites, inviting wicked spirits into our world."

Lucas grimaced. "Some creatures linger, awaiting chances to regain dominion. Every twelfth year their power peaks if rituals reopen the way." His finger stopped beneath a crude drawing of star-robed acolytes before a birch copse. "That alignment comes on Samhain's eve, three nights hence."

Ingram and Simon exchanged uneasy glances. The timing aligned with the innkeeper's warning. Ingram's fists clenched, readying for battle. "How can we stop this summoning?"

Brother Lucas lifted the torch higher. "The stars are not wholly aligned against us. Samhain's power flows both ways—gateways can also banish." His mouth curled in a sly grin that seemed out of place on his ascetic features. "With the proper ritual at a focus of ancient power, we may exorcise these devils for another age."

Ingram pondered this revelation. Though harnessing pagan ways felt dangerous, far worse would be allowing whatever evil stirred here to break its chains. Sometimes salvation came by walking the narrow path between order and chaos.

He turned to Lucas. "Tell us what you propose, and we shall lend our hands to the task."

The monk nodded. "Come. We prepare."

Chapter Fifteen

They spent that day and the next gathered around faded parchments, studying all known wisdom on the ritual ahead. Ingram immersed himself in dusty sigils and obscure chants late into the night. Brother Lucas proved a stern but erudite teacher, sharing insights no others living possessed. Ingram sensed a keen intelligence and curiosity beneath the monk's zealotry. Their goals aligned for now against a shared foe.

When the stars showed midnight had come on Samhain's eve, Lucas doused all lights in the crypt. "The hour approaches. We must reach the glen prepared to battle whatever has crossed over." He turned to Simon. "Are you ready, boy?"

Simon nodded fiercely, hand on the pommel of his family's storied longsword. Ingram set a steadying hand on his shoulder. Though untested, the lad's courage could tip the scales in their favor this night.

Filed out in dark robes, the three slipped through the empty courtyards past the chapel until the abbey wall loomed overhead. They gathered at an unmarked postern gate; its timbers wrapped with warding chains. Lucas drew a heavy key and unlocked the creaking door, gesturing them into the chilled darkness beyond.

The full moon broke through scudding clouds to reveal a pale ribbon of trail extending straight into the ominous forest. Lucas lit a shuttered lantern against soul-leeching entities and led the way into those shadowed reaches. The tangled woods embraced them, needled claws plucking at their woolen cloaks. Too soon the comforting lights of the abbey faded, leaving only a narrow glow to beat back primeval terrors pressing close on all sides.

When the straining gloom finally gave way to a moonlit clearing, Ingram nearly staggered in relief. Massive standing stones encircled the stark space, casting long shadows like a ring of silent sentinels. But they were not alone. Behind the ritual pillars, dozens of robed figures stood with heads raised to the cold heavens. An unearthly chant rolled forth, the syllables scraping like rough stones against Ingram's thoughts.

At a final bellowed exhortation, the cultists drew curved daggers and slashed their exposed arms in unison. Blood spattered the grove like dark rain. The scarlet droplets sizzled where they landed on the central white stone. Steam rose as deep cracks appeared across its surface. A rent gaped upward, pulsing red in sync with the surrounding chant. The cultists' eyes glowed feverishly as they presided over the widening portal. Soon, something would emerge from the abyssal tear.

With a savage cry, Lucas hurtled from the tree line brandishing a mace consecrated for crushing evil. Two cultists dropped before any reacted to the frenzied assault. Ingram and Simon drew weapons and charged to support him against the shocked believers. Lucas fought like one possessed, mace shattering bones and lives with reckless force. Ingram struck to disarm and disable where he could, unwilling to slaughter the misguided.

Simon fought to restrain a fleeing cultist. The robed man suddenly went rigid, back arching and teeth gnashing. *"You are too late,"* he choked in a guttural voice. Black liquid spilled from his contorting mouth as the entity inside him spoke. *"The gate has opened...they come..."*

With a final spasm, purple smoke erupted from the cultist's mouth before he collapsed lifeless. Simon scrambled away from the tainted corpse, face deathly pale. Ingram gripped his shoulder, staring in dismay toward the bloodstained stone. Several pairs of clawed, scaly hands reached through the steaming portal, grasping for purchase. The chanting became a frenzied screeching.

Lucas staggered to the altar, covered in gore and mace hanging limply. "The gates remain open while blood flows freely," he panted. Raising the mace high, he slammed it down, shattering the reddened pillars. The portal collapsed in a violent implosion, sucking the emerging demons back into darkness. Cracks continued spreading across the defiled altar as its unholy link broke.

Abruptly the chanting ceased as cultists cried out in pain and shock, clutching their heads. The trance broken, many fled wailing into the woods. Their master would be most displeased at this failure. But Ingram had no time for pursuit.

With a final grinding crack, the central pillar split completely. Lucas leapt aside as the two halves toppled slowly outward. The bloodied halves impacted the ground with a heavy thud that shook the clearing. Ingram watched tensely for further evil to emerge from the ruptured gate. But only an awful silence lingered.

Lucas spat in disgust. "Shoddy workmanship. But your arrival may have saved us all this night." He wiped his mace clean with a twist of his robe. "Gather the wounded. We must secure the abbey before the survivors come back."

Ingram glanced uneasily at the shattered altar. "First, we should consecrate this ground again. I don't trust whatever forces were unleashed here."

Lucas waved impatiently. "There will be time for that later. I must interrogate the prisoners for answers." An intense gleam shone in his eyes as he stared toward the compound. Ingram recognized the darkness lining that gaze. He prayed Lucas had not gazed overlong into the abyss they fought against. Sometimes the greater danger came from within.

Ingram stepped in front of Lucas, blocking his path back through the woods. "Brother, a moment. I share your desire for truth, but doubt these cultists hold any. Most seem mere thralls to some greater power." He glanced meaningfully at the scattered bodies. "Exercising temperance shows wisdom."

Lucas bristled, gripping his mace tighter. Ingram tensed but forced a conciliatory tone. "Please, holy father. Allow me to tend the wounded here with Simon while you secure the abbey. Quickly send more brothers so we may properly consecrate this unholy site." He held Lucas's fanatic gaze. "Vengeance can wait for dawn's light. Our priority must be shielding the innocent."

The monk slowly unclenched his weapon, a shred of reason tempering his fury. "You speak wisdom, my friend. I shall do as you advise." His sunken eyes looked haunted. "But do not tarry here. Darkness still congregates in these woods." Turning sharply, Lucas strode for the abbey, callously shoving the moaning cultists from his path.

Ingram watched him depart with growing unease. He hoped the monks could temper Lucas's vengeful spirit, lest it carry him into shadow. For now, they had injured prisoners to tend and ceremonial work ahead.

Gesturing Simon over, Ingram set him to gathering discarded robes to stanch the wounded. Despite his disgust, the lad obeyed, wincing as he wrapped makeshift tourniquets over gruesome gashes. Fortunately, most cultists had already fled. Ingram murmured softly to the ones too dazed to move, checking pupils and pulses. He knew enough of physic arts to clean and bind the deeper cuts. The rest would have to mend through prayer and Providence.

As he worked, Ingram studied the remaining monoliths encircling them. Crude figures and glyphs depicted horned entities accepting elaborate offerings and supplications. Such profane iconography lent the clearing a lingering miasma. They must purify this area without delay.

Heavy footsteps heralded the arrival of a half-dozen monks carrying blessed candles, books, and relics. Ingram instructed them gently but firmly, and soon solemn chanting filled the grove, battling lingering darkness. When the last rites finished, a breath of dawn's promise stirred the still air. Ingram finally allowed fatigue to seep into his bones. They had won a deep victory here, though at grave cost.

With the monks' aid, Ingram and Simon transported the wounded back to the abbey's infirmary where their cultist brands could be treated discreetly. Lucas was blessedly absent, presumably reporting to the abbot and reinforcing the abbey's security. Ingram recommended posting trusted brothers in the forest to intercept any returning acolytes.

As he finally exited the cellar sickrooms, Ingram nearly stumbled over a slight, sandy-haired boy scrubbing the floors.

The lad froze like a startled animal when Ingram bent to help him up. The pure innocence in his frightened eyes wrenched Ingram's heart. What had circumstances forced this child to witness in life?

"Here now, easy," Ingram soothed, slowing his movements. "I won't harm you." He kept his tone gentle. "I'm called Ingram. What's your name?"

The boy hesitated. "Corey, sir. I keep the floors and fires here." He nervously eyed Ingram's stained tunic. "Are you sore wounded?"

Ingram smiled. "No, I managed to duck quicker than the other fellows. It's their blood." He pretended to examine himself critically. "Though I am rather filthy. Think your floors could survive me visiting the washroom?"

Corey bit his lip. "Well, I just scrubbed them..." Seeing Ingram's melancholy sigh, he managed a shy smile. "Oh, I suppose I can scrub them again. This way." He gestured down the hall. Ingram shot him a grateful wink before following.

The simple rituals of washing grime and gore away restored Ingram's equilibrium. Donning a fresh novice's robe, he rejoined Corey in the corridor. "I feel a new man. Now, I don't know about you, but I could use some breakfast after the night we've had."

Soon Ingram was sitting in the kitchen watching Corey enthusiastically polish off a bowl of porridge. Ingram slid his portion over when the scrawny lad eyed it hungrily. Between servings, he asked about the boy's history here, keeping his tone gently casual.

"Wasn't always like this," Corey mumbled around a mouthful of oats. "I helped make candles and soaps once. But since the wood went dark, everyone's afraid all the time. The brothers argue instead of praying." He ducked his head. "I try not to listen."

Ingram's jaw tightened. He rested a tentative hand on Corey's bony shoulder. "You're very brave staying when so many left. This place needs souls like you who focus on their work and have faith."

Corey peeked up hesitantly. "You really think so? The others said I was too small to join them defending the abbey." His face fell. "I only know how to polish and pray."

"All tasks done well please God," Ingram said firmly. "Just hold to the virtues He instilled in you, and you cannot go far wrong."

Rising stiffly, he nodded to the boy. "I should go speak with the abbot now. Will you bring me more hot water later for a bath?"

Corey nodded eagerly. "Of course, sir! I will work extra hard."

Ingram smiled as he departed, warmed by the encounter. Despite the innocent suffering evil caused, it could not corrupt every soul or sever humanity's innate bonds. He must hold on to that truth which transcended doctrine or creeds. If goodness remained in one faithful heart, hope endured.

Chapter Sixteen

Brooding monks watched Ingram's approach to the abbot's study with dark suspicion. But a sharp word from inside bade him enter. The abbot sat erect behind a heavy table carved with symbols of order and wisdom. Gray owl's wings of hair framed his careworn face, but keen intelligence still burned in his gaze.

"Welcome, traveler. Brother Lucas tells me we owe you a great debt this night."

Ingram bowed slightly. "I played but a small role, Father. Though I am glad Providence placed me here in your time of need."

The abbot gestured to a stool. "Providence, or something more? Our troubles began when Lucas returned from his pilgrimage, changed. Some poison touched his spirit." He searched Ingram's face. "I discern you too have walked in shadow."

Ingram remained silent as the abbot continued. "Do not misjudge me...I would embrace any penitent who brought light. But these are uncertain times. Tell me, what truly guided you to us?"

Bowing his head, Ingram haltingly described his recent crusade freeing the mountain village from vampiric evil. "Since then, I have wandered, seeking purpose. When whispers reached me of this abbey's plight, I knew my road led here." He met the abbot's eyes earnestly. "I aim only to serve those who need deliverance from darkness."

The abbot considered his words. "A worthy aspiration if it holds true." He steepled his fingers. "I shall watch your deeds here closely to better understand your character. For now, know that you and young Simon may remain and assist...within limits."

Ingram bowed deeply. "You show much grace, Father. We shall prove ourselves allies to peace."

A loud clamor in the courtyard startled them both. The abbot frowned. "Hasty shouts also accompany Brother Lucas of late. Go see what stirs our uneasy flock this time."

Ingram exited the study to find Lucas and a handful of monks clustered around a small building set apart from the main compound. Ironbound oak reinforced the squat stone structure with only a few shuttered slits for light. From within came muffled shouts and vicious pounding.

Lucas turned to Ingram with feverish eyes. "The prisoner awaits questioning. I had her placed in the penitent's cell." He gestured impatiently to the monks. "Quickly, undo these locks so we may begin."

Ingram stepped nearer warily. A young woman's desperate screams echoed from within those merciless walls. They conjured vivid memories of his grandmother's tales about the tortured "witches" held in such cells.

"Father, perhaps we should consider—" he began gently.

Lucas's eyes flashed. "You question me? You who arrived unbidden on these pagan rites?" He lifted his mace menacingly. "I will discover what powers corrupted our sanctuary, one way or another."

The monk's supporters growled approvingly and moved to unbar the door beneath the shrieking prisoner's frantic blows.

Ingram stepped forward placatingly as Lucas made to enter the cell containing the hysterical prisoner.

"Brother, surely this woman was but a misguided pawn in evil's scheme," he implored. "Would not gentle guidance steer her truer than threats and torment?"

Lucas whirled, eyes aflame. "You forget your place, stranger. These heretics nearly unleashed doom upon us all!" He gestured sharply for the monks to continue opening the door. "I shall learn what corrupted them, by honeyed words or harsher means."

Seeing reason would not deter zealotry, Ingram sprang forward and grabbed Lucas's arm. "I cannot stand idle while you torture the innocent!"

With a grunt of effort, he hurled the monk back from the cell entrance. Lucas careened into his supporters, sending them sprawling. By the time they untangled themselves, Ingram had hauled a wooden bench over to block the door.

Lucas surged to his feet, face mottled with rage. "How dare you lay hands on me! I am vested by the abbot himself to root out evil by any righteous means." He stalked toward Ingram, spittle flying as he shouted. "Step aside, heretic, or be deemed as tainted as she!"

Ingram stood his ground. "I know only that we must meet darkness with light or forfeit our own souls." He kept his voice calm but firm. "I cannot let a servant of God succumb to cruelty, whatever the cause."

For a moment Lucas trembled, torn between clashing impulses. Ingram braced for an attack, but gradual realization tempered the monk's fury. With a snarl, Lucas turned and marched off, supporters trailing in confusion. Ingram waited until they had gone before sagging in relief. Perhaps wisdom had intervened, but he did not know how long this unstable peace could last.

The woman's shrieks inside the cell had given way to hoarse weeping. Ingram called out gently, "Take heart, mistress. None shall harm you now. What is your name?"

There was silence except her ragged breathing. Then a tremulous voice answered. "E–Eliza, sir. Are they gone?"

"For the moment. But you are not safe here," Ingram replied grimly. "Do you know of any hidden way out?"

More silence. Then, footsteps scuffed toward the door. "There is a way, sir. Please let me out."

Ingram hesitated. She could be lying in hopes of escaping. But leaving her locked in this crypt ran contrary to his conscience. And if he lingered here much longer, Lucas might return with the abbot's sanction. That left only one path.

Bracing his shoulder against the solid door, Ingram heaved the bench aside. He lifted the crossbar and pulled the creaking portal open. From the gloom, a slight, disheveled young woman peered up at him. The faded robes she wore were smeared with dirt and blood. But her face shone with innocent hope.

"Bless you, sir. I only wish to be free of this dread place." She glanced around fearfully. "The monk, Lucas—he frightens me."

Ingram offered his hand. "Come, we must move quickly and quietly now."

Eliza allowed him to lead her across the compound into the shadow of a dilapidated workshop. Ingram hoped tools left here could help force a little–used postern gate he had spied earlier. But sudden shouts and ringing blades shattered the lonely gloom. Ingram turned to see Lucas charging at the head of a dozen armed monks. Their foaming leader glared pure malice.

"Seize the heretic and his witch!"

Ingram shoved Eliza towards the back of the shed. "Bar the door and flee if you can! I will hold them off." Drawing his sword, he turned to face the frenzied mob.

Lucas attacked first, his mace smashing aside Ingram's parry and grazing his shoulder. Grunting in pain, Ingram gave ground before the onslaught. He cursed himself for leaving his blessed weapons back in the crypt. But perhaps words could yet succeed where steel failed.

"Brothers, stay your hands!" he implored, ducking another vicious swing from Lucas. "This woman has not received the abbot's justice yet."

That gave some of the monks pause. But Lucas was deaf to reason. He battered at Ingram's guard, spitting vitriol between breaths. "Deceiving serpent! You revealed your true master when you interfered with God's work."

The monks encircled the dueling pair, restless for the heretic's blood. Ingram silently prayed for forgiveness over what he must do. When Lucas overextended on his next wild swing, Ingram seized his wrist and pulled him into a savage headbutt. Cartilage crunched wetly.

Howling, Lucas staggered back clutching his gushing nose. Ingram swiftly disarmed two of his shocked supporters and leveled their blades at the rest.

"Do not force my hand any further," he warned. "Throw down your weapons."

But fervor overruled prudence. With a bellow, the monks attacked as one. Ingram traded fierce blows, using his opponents' numbers against them. When one left him an opening, Ingram pressed it ruthlessly. Soon a pile of groaning, unconscious forms littered the ground.

A crazed shout made Ingram turn just in time to lift his blade, catching Lucas's mace swing short. His muscles strained as zealotry lent the mad monk uncanny force. Ingram struggled for leverage in the uneven footing. If he faltered, the spiked mace would crush his skull like an overripe melon.

With a desperate heave, Ingram slid his sword down Lucas's haft, trapping the weapon against the ground. Before Lucas could relinquish his grip, Ingram snatched a fallen blade and slammed the hilt into his temple. The monk's eyes rolled back and he dropped boneless to the earth.

Chest heaving, Ingram staggered free of the bodies. The postern gate stood tantalizingly close now. He hurried to the shed where Eliza still huddled.

"Hurry, we must go before they revive," he urged. But as she rose into the light, Ingram froze. For the first time, he glimpsed defined features under her matted hair. They stirred a strange familiarity, like a recurring dream.

Those wide eyes...had he known them once in another life?

Ingram shook off the impression. No time for flights of fancy now. He took Eliza's hand and led her quickly to the small gate. The heavy bar resisted his weakened arms, but finally creaked open. Beckoning Eliza through, Ingram pulled it shut behind them. Then they hurried into the concealing trees beyond the abbey walls.

Stumbling over roots and stones, they scrambled down into a ravine filled with deadfalls. Only when the abbey towers disappeared behind the ridge did Ingram signal a halt. Gulping icy stream water and gasping for breath, they finally slowed their panicked flight. Ingram peeled back Eliza's tattered sleeve to reveal a long bleeding scratch, likely caught during their wild escape. He tore a strip from his own robe to bandage it.

"What now?" Eliza gasped, wide eyes surveying the shadowy forest surrounding them. "If they catch us..."

Ingram squeezed her shoulder. "Do not despair. Once tempers cool, reason may yet prevail." Even as he said it, Ingram wondered if peace were possible now. Perhaps the only path was ensuring those innocents caught in the center came to no harm.

"Rest here. I'm going to find Simon so we can leave this place together." He scraped a rudimentary map in the dirt. "Follow this stream north until you reach a shepherd's hut. Hide there until I come."

Eliza nodded mutely, huddled on the streambank looking small and afraid. Ingram hesitated, then removed his crucifix and draped it around her neck. "Keep this close. It will protect your spirit."

Impulsively he leaned down to gently kiss Eliza's grimy forehead. "Have faith. This darkness will pass."

Before she could respond, Ingram slipped off into the gnarled trees. Tracking the abbey's spires in the distance, he began circumnavigating back toward the front gates. He had to find Simon and make for Gault before Lucas could muster a larger hunting party. Ingram prayed their presence had done more good than ill, but the fallen monk's fanaticism complicated that equation. They needed to bring the abbot full tidings of events before more chaos erupted.

Careful of lingering patrols, Ingram crept up to the main abbey road. From concealment he whistled the soft nightingale call he and Simon used as a signal. When it went unanswered, he risked stealing closer to the gatehouse. No lamps burned atop the parapets. The whole compound appeared darkened and still.

Unease skittered down Ingram's spine. Had the abbot ordered a lights-out curfew? Or were more sinister preparations underway? As he studied the facade for any clues, a subtle whistle came from the shadow of a covered wagon by the front gate. Ingram whistled back and Simon emerged, hurrying over.

"Thank the saints! I already feared you were discovered or imprisoned," the youth exclaimed, embracing Ingram tightly.

Ingram quickly explained the confrontation with Lucas and subsequent escape. "We cannot delay. The abbot may listen to reason, but Brother Lucas seemed beyond hearing any but the whispers in his head."

Simon spat. "That dog! He raved to the monks, claiming you were a heretic and sorcerer." His face fell. "They searched the whole abbey, so I fled here to wait for you."

Ingram gripped his shoulder. "You did well. Come, we shall take the high road for Gault. You still have kin there who can aid us?"

Simon nodded firmly. "None who would turn away family. We shall be welcome."

Together they crept past ditches and walls until the abbey was lost to sight. The road ahead remained open for leagues before the next village. Ingram said a silent prayer of thanks that they had escaped the compound without raising an alarm. Perhaps church justice could yet resolve this without further lives being ruined.

Chapter Seventeen

The full moon broke through scudding clouds, lighting their way between towering oak and ash groves. Ingram guessed it was nearing midnight, but weariness could not yet touch his pounding heart and spinning thoughts. Glancing over, he saw Simon's lips moving in silent prayer, doubtless also seeking calm. But sudden flickering lights ahead stole any fragile peace.

Through the trees candle flames bobbed and wove as voices called out. Ingram and Simon hastily dove off the road, scrambling into the dense thicket. Ingram risked peering between the branches as the commotion drew closer. Riders surrounded a simple wagon bearing a covered load. The leader held up a torch, illuminating his sharp–boned features. Lucas.

Ingram's belly turned to ice. There could be only one reason for Lucas to lead armed men from the abbey by night. Ingram watched helplessly as the procession jounced past their hiding spot. But as the wagon trundled by, the wind stirred its woven covering. Slender, bound hands dangled lifelessly from the edge.

Ingram stifled a cry as he recognized Eliza's torn and dirtied sleeve. His stomach rebelled at the implications. They must have traced her path and ripped her from whatever brief sanctuary she had found. Now Lucas bore his captive back in triumph to whatever twisted judgment awaited.

Guilt and rage churned bitterly within Ingram. He never should have involved the poor girl in his feud with the deranged monk. Now her blood and pain would be on his hands if he did not somehow intervene.

Gesturing urgently to Simon, Ingram scrambled from the thicket and raced back up the road. There might yet be a chance to thwart Lucas before he brought more suffering onto that blameless soul. Ingram refused to stand idle while the innocent suffered because of actions he had set in motion. Some fates were too cruel even to risk.

He heard Simon gaining behind as Ingram pushed his aching body to its limit. Ahead, the bobbing lights had disappeared around a bend. As they raced after, Ingram tried desperately to form some plan with his exhausted mind. Lucas could not be allowed to reach the abbey gates again. Nor could Eliza remain his helpless captive. Ingram prayed fervently that God would guide his hand one final time.

Rounding the bend, he spied the procession less than a hundred yards ahead. Ingram drove himself even faster. There was only one way to stop them in time. Gripping the small crucifix tied round his wrist, Ingram lowered his shoulder and roared a desperate battle cry.

Startled shouts came from the convoy. Riders struggled to turn their mounts before Ingram crashed into the rear cart. Wood splintered violently and Ingram spilled onto the rocky road. For a brief moment all was chaos. Then Ingram glimpsed Eliza's limp hands dragging the ground just out of reach. Scrambling desperately, he seized her wrists, hauled her body free from the wreckage, and carried her over his shoulder.

Simon arrived brandishing his sword wildly to hold off the stunned pursuers. "Move, quickly!" Ingram shouted. Simon retreated step by step, keeping the riders at bay. Just as they broke free to run, a taloned bolt pierced Simon's thigh. He cried out and stumbled, but Ingram caught him. Half-dragging the lad, they crashed off the road into the woods. More bolts whistled past, but soon they were shielded by gnarled trunks and dense brush.

Ingram gently lay Eliza and Simon in the shelter of an ancient oak. The young woman was bound hand and foot, with dark stains marring her robes. But her chest rose faintly with breath. Bowstrings thrummed out on the road as Ingram swiftly tended to Simon. The bolt had gone clean through muscle without hitting bone. Once the bleeding was stanched, Simon waved off any more aid.

"We have to keep moving, before they trap us here," he panted, letting Ingram pull him upright. Turning, they cut Eliza's bonds and administered water from their skins. Her eyelids fluttered open fearfully. At the sight of Ingram, relief broke over her face.

"You came for me?" she whispered in wonder. Then her eyes widened. "Look out!"

Ingram spun, sword meeting the swooping blade just in time. One of Lucas's scouts had crept up on their position. Steel sparked as they exchanged vicious blows. Ingram fell back under a series of blinding strikes. As he tripped over an exposed root, his foe raised a sword for the killing stroke.

A rock bounced off the monk's head, making him stagger. Ingram seized the distraction to drive his blade into the man's chest. Wide eyes met his as the monk sagged against him, breath rattling wetly. Ingram lowered the body down with shaking hands.

"God forgive me," he murmured over the still form. Looking up, he saw Eliza holding another rock, staring in shock. Simon leaned heavily against the oak, face pale. Ingram cleaned his sword, sighing wearily.

"We must go. More will be along shortly." He glanced at Eliza sadly. "I fear you are marked for some terrible fate as long as you travel with us."

She gripped his arm, eyes determined through lingering fear. "I trust you, not them. Please, let me stay by your side."

Ingram swallowed thickly, then nodded. "Stay close then." They moved deeper into the moon-dappled woods. Some paths led yet to gentler places if one had courage and faith to walk in hope.

The night crept on as the three limped westward, seeking any refuge. Ingram had stopped the scouts, but the delay gave them a slim margin of time before the main party resumed their relentless pursuit. He strained every sense against the quiet forest, flinching at shadows. Yet strangely, nothing stirred around them save the sigh of night winds.

His nerves screamed it was a trap, but they had no choice but to keep limping doggedly onward. Ingram watched helplessly as Simon fell farther behind, leaning on trees to stay upright. His bandaged leg left a spotty trail of black blood despite Ingram's best efforts. Even Eliza struggled not to collapse, though she made no sound of complaint. Ingram did what little he could to help them along, mouth dry with fear and weariness.

Finally, Simon's legs could bear no more. He sunk to the mossy trunk of a lightning–split oak, breathing in ragged gasps. Ingram quickly scanned their surroundings. They seemed to be in a small hollow surrounded by hawthorn trees. The rocky soil offered little shelter, but overhanging branches would have to suffice.

"Rest here awhile to gather strength," he murmured, though dawn could not be far off now. "I will keep watch."

Eliza helped Simon sip from a water skin before the lad slipped into exhausted slumber. Then she joined Ingram at the hollow's edge, staring out into the shadowed woods. They sat without speaking as the sky lightened to pearl gray. Ingram silently recited the divine offices, clinging to the familiar ritual amidst chaos. Beside him, Eliza murmured soft prayers, rocking gently like a child seeking comfort.

As gold touched the highest branches, birdsong broke the stillness. Ingram felt Eliza stiffen beside him at the sound of heavier footsteps tramping through the underbrush. He rose, sword scraping from its sheath. But instead of armored monks, only a lone gray wolf emerged from between the trunks. Regarding them with gleaming eyes, the elder beast dipped its head once before melting back into the murmuring wilds.

Ingram released a shaky breath, envying the creature's easy freedom. But surrender was not yet theirs. Hefting Simon's arm over his shoulder, Ingram gently roused the bleeding lad. "We have to keep moving," he whispered. "Stay with us."

Together they staggered up out of the hollow, no destination but away from their pursuers. As the woods thinned atop a modest rise, Eliza gasped and pointed shakily. There in the distance, wisps of chimney smoke rose above humble thatched roofs. A small village nestled in the valley below. At the sight, Ingram felt tears prick his smoke–reddened eyes. Sanctuary beckoned for their battered fellowship.

With renewed vigor they pressed on, skirting fields and walls until a narrow lane deposited them in the town's center. Villagers paused in their morning rounds to eye the ragged trio limping painfully into their midst. Ingram knew they made quite the spectacle.

Spotting the alehouse, he steered Simon and Eliza toward its doors still shuttered against the dawn. The commotion brought a tousled matron bustling outside, scolding sticking in her throat when she spied Ingram's party. Her eyes widened at the blood and grime marking their haggard faces.

Ingram fished a few coins from his robe. "Please, we require rest and discretion if you can spare it."

The innkeeper's face softened. She ushered them inside without a word, bolting the door before seeing to their injuries herself. Soon Ingram collapsed on a straw pallet watching blearily as she tended each companion in turn. Her name was Bronwen, he learned when exhaustion loosened his tongue. A widow running her late husband's tavern and trying to shield two young sons from the world's harsh lessons.

"We attract more than our share of trouble here along the drover's road. I'll not pry into your business," Bronwen murmured, dabbing salve on Ingram's torn shoulder. "The little room upstairs is yours long as needed. I'll bring broth when you wake."

She glanced at Eliza already curled up asleep beside the hearth. "Poor lamb. Those scoundrels ought to be strung up for hurting a lass." Meeting Ingram's haunted eyes, her look softened. "You rest easy now. Beneath my roof, you're safe as in your mother's arms."

Ingram could only nod wearily. But those comforting words released tears too long swallowed. As she gently brushed back his hair like his grandmother had done lifetimes ago, the dispossessed wanderer wept. Not only for recent trauma, but a bone-deep grief over losing any sense of home or sanctuary. Through his tears, Ingram glimpsed the first rays of hope dawning in a decade of darkness.

When Ingram next awoke, a ruddy sunset glowed through the room's single window. Downstairs he found Bronwen serving hearty stews to a handful of locals. Ingram's stomach rumbled, reminding him it had been days since real food or comfort had sustained his body and spirit. Sliding onto a bench, he let the inn's warmth seep into his tired bones. Here, no one eyed him with suspicion or malice. Just simple acceptance of another soul needing rest.

Soon Simon limped down to join him, moving gingerly but with some color in his cheeks again. Ingram clasped the lad's shoulder, sharing a weary smile. They had survived the worst and regained a light to guide them from the brink of despair. Whatever silver still lined Ingram's pockets, they owed all of it to Bronwen's rare kindness.

Eliza remained abed, recovering from invisible torments. But Bronwen assured Ingram the lass just needed more rest and care. In time, her spirit would heal as well. Ingram prayed it was so. Seeing innocence shattered wounded his own soul. Protecting what fragile joy remained must be their mission now.

Over the next few days, Ingram regained his strength splitting logs and doing minor repairs around the tavern. Avoiding uneasy questions let him fade into the passing crowd of peddlers, craftsmen, and tradesmen dependent on Bronwen's hospitality. By unspoken agreement, the peace was not disturbed by digging into his past. The present moment held blessings enough.

When chores allowed, Ingram checked on Eliza's progress. Color gradually returned to her cheeks, and she no longer woke screaming from nightmares. But she had not ventured outside or spoken since their arrival. Ingram sat with her when he could, sometimes reading scripture, other times just holding her work–worn hand in silent companionship. The light would return to her eyes someday if given patience and care. He had faith.

Late one afternoon, Ingram entered the musty chapel adjoining Bronwen's inn seeking solitude. Kneeling before the crude altar, he let weariness overtake his thoughts. So much violence and chaos lately in the name of courage and conviction. How was one to stay the righteous path in a world so rife with suffering? What was just cause, and what only poisonous vengeance? The questions weighed on Ingram's soul.

A timid footstep at the doorway startled him from introspection. Turning, he saw Eliza outlined in the setting sun's glow. She hesitated on the threshold as if fearing to commit some sacrilege. Beckoning gently, Ingram invited her to share the pew's solace.

After a moment she joined him, staring at the hands folded in her lap. A comfortable silence embraced them, two souls seeking meaning together. Then Eliza spoke, voice fragile as the sighing wind.

"I feel so...lost. Everything I believed is gone." She finally lifted her head, searching Ingram's face beseechingly. "Why do such evil men seem to hold all the power? What justice could allow what he did..." Tears welled in her eyes but did not fall.

Ingram chose his words carefully. "I do not know why Providence seems to permit innocents to suffer. But I have faith that in time, all shadows must yield to the coming dawn." Gently he took her hand. "We cannot surrender hope because of others' cruelty. Within us lies the power to create the world anew, one heart at a time."

Eliza's fingers tightened on his. "My heart feels too broken. I cannot forget the things I saw." She shuddered, lost in evil memories.

Turning her palm over, Ingram traced a delicate cross. "Here is light to guide you from those dark visions." He smiled sadly. "I too have seen such terrible things. But even one act of love redeems whole worlds of suffering."

Fresh tears brimmed in Eliza's eyes. Then wonder dawned on her face as the first drops traced glistening trails down her cheeks. Raising a hand to catch them, she whispered in awe, "I can...cry again. My heart was too cold before."

She embraced Ingram fiercely then, weeping freely for the first time since her ordeal. He held her close, letting compassion flow between them. If one soul could shed tears again, then hope endured for all creation. They had only to kindle that flame wherever darkness tried to extinguish the spark.

When Eliza's sobs finally ceased, she pulled back self–consciously dabbing her eyes with a kerchief. But serenity softened her features now. "You've given me a great gift," she murmured. "I want to help bring that light to others lost in shadow. Will you teach me?"

Joy surged in Ingram's chest. "It would be my honor. We shall walk in hope together."

Standing in the fading sunlight, they shook hands solemnly. Then arm in arm, the wounded healer and renewed spirit walked forward to share dinner with good folk awaiting them. No matter the trials ahead, they would face them as one.

Chapter Eighteen

Spring came late to the high country, but its arrival washed away the last clinging shadows of winter's tyranny. Swelling buds adorned the trees edging Bronwen's modest tavern yard, and raucous birdsong filled the dawn air. Looking out the dew-limned window of his snug chamber, Ingram breathed deep the scents of renewal. For a brief time, they had found a pocket of peace to mend body and soul before continuing their ceaseless quest.

Downstairs, the morning crowd had already gathered to break their fasts with hot oats and yesterday's bread. Bronwen stirred an iron pot of porridge between serving round after round of ale to the valley locals here more for gossip and company than her admittedly average cuisine. But the tavern food filled bellies, and its rustic warmth healed less tangible hunger.

Ingram sat quietly absorbing the environment. After a lifetime moving ever onward, he was learning the humble joy in stillness and ordinary community. A port in the storm carried its own riches. As Bronwen passed with a basket of eggs, Ingram gently touched her wrist.

"Bless you for all you've done," he said plainly. "We can never fully repay this kindness."

She colored slightly but patted Ingram's hand. "Seeing you all healed and smiling is payment enough." Glancing at Eliza who was kneading dough for fresh bread, her eyes misted slightly. "It's how my boys should remember me when I'm gone: as one who helped carry others through dark nights of the soul."

Just then the door crashed open to admit a blast of crisp air and two lanky, tow-headed teens. Freshly back from their morning's work, they hurried to kiss Bronwen's flushed cheek and steal bites of breakfast. Watching them, Ingram marveled at this microcosm of humanity thriving simply by sustaining one another through compassion. If such pockets of light endured, darkness could never claim total victory.

After the meal, Ingram prepared to depart for the day's work assisting nearby homesteads and shops. The laborers and peddlers who frequented Bronwen's inn seemed to accept his help without prying into his past. Ingram offered aid wherever needed in thanks for the sanctuary granted. He understood such reprieve could be fleeting for wandering souls.

Simon emerged gingerly from the back room to join him. Though his leg still pained him, the stout youth chafed at inaction. Together they had regained some strength and peace in this rustic haven. Perhaps Simon could find purpose again in a life of simple community rather than violence. Ingram secretly hoped the boy would choose to remain here rather than continue down his lonely path. These gentle folk needed spirited help to flourish.

They strolled the greening lane sharing idle thoughts and observations. Spring peepers trilled from every pond and ditch, heralding life's resurgence. Outside the valley, some men still played petty tyrant. But beneath the open sky, hope's rhythm endured eternal.

Pausing atop a gentle rise, the pair contemplated the patchwork of cleared fields and woodlots comprising the village. Thin smoke rose from a charcoal kiln in the oak groves to the south. Closer by, children laughed while driving small flocks to pasture. Such humble pastoral moments had sustained humanity since ancient days.

Simon broke the companionable silence. "It's beautiful country, but part of me already yearns for the road. Does that make me restless or ungrateful?"

Ingram clapped his shoulder. "It means you are young, with an appetite for adventure. I was the same once." He sighed regretfully. "Stay awhile longer before rushing back into peril. Wisdom comes slowly to our kind."

"Yet if your crusade taught me anything, it's that we each have a purpose," Simon insisted. "One cannot simply hide away when evil still shadows the land." His jaw clenched with renewed conviction. "I should be helping you fight it, as we did before."

Ingram's rebuttal froze as shrieks drifted up from the valley. Exchanging an alarmed glance with Simon, he broke into a run down the tree–lined lane. The sound swelled as they drew nearer, carried by villagers fleeing up the path from the village center. Children wailed while women gathered their skirts and elderly limped along, terror etched on their faces.

Reaching the village green, Ingram skidded to a halt at the unfolding scene. Bronwen stood resolute before her inn, apron clutched to her breast. Her eyes remained defiant though Ingram glimpsed tear tracks on her flour–dusted cheeks.

Before Bronwen stood a ring of mounted, mailed men wearing purple livery emblazoned with a golden hawk emblem.

In their midst knelt her two sons, hands bound as a soldier held a sword's blade to the older boy's exposed neck. More soldiers emerged from the inn, dragging a bound Eliza between them. At the tavern yard's edge sprawled a limp figure leaking blood into the new spring grass. One of Bronwen's patrons struck down defending the sanctuary he'd found there.

Ingram reached for the sword he no longer carried, cursing himself. Righteous fury boiled up to cut down these brigands accosting innocents. But there were so many heavily armed soldiers between him and the prisoners. Any violent rescue attempt would end in more innocent bloodshed.

A man on a pale warhorse watched the proceedings dispassionately. But Ingram recognized those sharp features and sunken eyes. He prayed he was wrong even as icy talons clutched his racing heart. It could not be him. Not here.

The noble glanced Ingram's way. His eyes narrowed slightly in recognition, but no hint of surprise or anger touched his stoic features. He simply prodded his mount forward, chainmail jingling.

"Ingram of Gault," he intoned flatly. "You are far from where last we met."

Ingram's throat felt raw, but he kept outrage thickening his voice. "Lord Winton Ashcroft. Is this how you now treat wayfarers and widows in your domain?"

The knight sighed as if faced with a minor inconvenience. "I seek only to retrieve what is mine. The woman is a heretic wanted for trial and abjuration. Sheltering apostates puts all here in peril." His sunken eyes bored into Ingram. "I suggest you move along and leave secular affairs of state to your betters."

Ingram did not budge from the path. "I cannot ignore injustice, whatever our past." He gestured sharply at the kneeling boys. "This is dishonor, not justice. Let them go."

Ashcroft glanced at the captives with detached appraisal. "Regret floods my heart, truly." His tone remained arctic. "But as you'll recall, I take a hard line against those who defy or subvert me."

He nodded at his sword-wielding lieutenant. "Teach them the cost."

Ingram roared in denial, shoving through the crowd. But he was too late. With merciless precision, the knight's blade slashed Bronwen's eldest son Heath from nape to breastbone. The youth crumpled, eyes wide with shock.

A wail tore from Bronwen as she flew to her slain boy. Eliza screamed and fought her captor's grip. Ashcroft watched it all with narrowed eyes, unmoved as stone. Ingram shook with helpless fury, knuckles bone white. What God forsook such monsters to prey freely on the innocent?

The lieutenant flipped his blade coolly. "Shall I continue instructing them?" Ashcroft raised a forestalling hand. Bronwen clung desperately to her child, keening grief ignored by the encircling men. At last Ashcroft met Ingram's enraged stare.

"Ride out. Pursue what destiny calls you. But know I shall now keep closer watch." Spurring his horse forward, he leaned down to grip Ingram's jaw. "Live ever glancing behind, heretic. My hand remains poised to smite all you hold dear."

Releasing him contemptuously, Lord Ashcroft turned his mount and called for the soldiers to move out. Rough hands hauled the survivors to their feet and shoved them along protesting. Within moments, the only sounds were Bronwen's anguished cries mixing with the sigh of wind through new spring leaves. Her surviving son stared after the departed soldiers in numb shock, eyes welling as her screams tore at his heart.

Ingram moved as if in a nightmare to embrace her shaking shoulders. But no words could penetrate the icy shroud wrapping her soul. Her wails held a purity of agony beyond any comfort he knew to give. What use was faith or wisdom in the face of such violence ripping lives asunder?

He looked up as Simon slowly approached, cheeks wet with tears of empathy. The youth knelt and gently helped draw Bronwen into the shelter of the inn that now felt violated. Ingram remained a while by the boy's body, watching his blood soak sluggishly into soil preparing to bring forth new life. The ways of evil confounded all reason or justice.

When he finally rose and walked leadenly inside, Ingram found the common room emptied by the horror. He began preparing the poor lad for burial, working through burning tears. Each kindness, no matter how small, was a blow struck against the encroaching dark. He would see this son to his rest with gentle rites. It was woefully insufficient, but all he could offer the bereft mother.

Ingram had no answers in the face of such vicious cruelty. But he refused to let darkness prevail uncontested. If their own hearts must serve as torches to light the way, so be it. This oppressive shadow demanded resistance, not surrender. They would tend this hallowed ground and continue spreading solace, come what horrors may.

Chapter Nineteen

In the pre-dawn stillness, Ingram kept solitary watch over Heath laid out upon the trestle table. A linen cloth covered his wound.

A creak on the stairs turned his head. Eliza paused at the periphery of the candlelight, her eyes twin wells of shadow. When Ingram said nothing, she approached to lay a timid hand on his slumped shoulder.

"You should rest," she murmured. "I will sit with him now."

Ingram started to protest, but the heaviness of his limbs betrayed his exhaustion. After Bronwen had finally slipped into tearful slumber, he had maintained this vigil alone, penance for failing to protect her child. But Eliza was right; he was in no state to aid the living or honor the dead. With a mute nod, he relinquished his post and trudged upstairs.

Collapsing into bed fully clothed, Ingram begged dreamless oblivion. But spectral faces gathered in his mind's eye, all those he had known briefly yet failed to save. Accusing glares bored into him. Why had he survived when so many worthier had not? Their silent condemnation mingled with half-remembered screams, dragging Ingram into feverish nightmares. He thrashed in the sweat-soaked sheets, haunted by all those souls his actions condemned through carelessness or inaction. In fitful visions he relived Bronwen's anguished cries as her beautiful boy bled out, steely hatred filling Lord

Ashcroft's sunken eyes. Somewhere his own voice pleaded uselessly for mercy while demonic shadows chortled.

Ingram jerked awake with a hoarse cry. Weak dawn light filtered through the chamber's dirt-clouded window, reflecting his own inner murkiness. For an empty moment he contemplated staying abed rather than facing the remains of happiness violated. But the living needed what feeble comfort he could provide. Personal grief must wait.

Stiffly Ingram rose and descended the creaking stair. In the common room, trestle tables had been pushed aside to make space for the plain casket and meager funeral trappings. Bronwen sat slump-shouldered staring down at her folded hands. Ingram hesitated to intrude on her grief, but she looked up with red–rimmed eyes.

"I would not have survived the night without Eliza's care," Bronwen rasped. "She prayed the hours away tirelessly while I wrestled demons in the dark."

Ingram nodded, unsurprised by Eliza's compassion. "I am here now. Let me take up the vigil for a time so you may rest."

Bronwen started to protest but surrendered to exhaustion. Her remaining son Aiken helped her limp up the stairs to lay down. Ingram turned to find Eliza sweeping the now empty hearth, motions slow and eyes downcast. He searched for words to salve her own sadness but found none that did not taste bitter. Sometimes silence carried the only wisdom.

Neighbors soon gathered, worn faces etched with solemn empathy. The local fathers muttered abbreviated rites from a tattered book of hours. Two men hefted the rude casket up onto their shoulders and shuffled toward the graveyard's weed-choked fence. The procession of weeping women and silent men seemed painfully small for one whose short life had touched so many hearts.

Ingram supported the devastated Aiken while dirt thudded down on his brother's grave. All reborn innocence and laughter stilled forever now. Aiken stared dry-eyed at the raw mound amidst toppled markers. Too numb for tears, the shock of loss had sealed away overwhelming grief for a time. Ingram knew that small mercy would fade all too quickly.

The subdued group lingered awhile, sharing murmured consolations and bracing embraces. But life's daily necessity soon drew them back to work and routine. Alone before the disturbed earth, Ingram whispered a prayer for the departed soul finding its way without kin and home. If any grace yet lingered, may it light that journey into shadow.

Turning back, he nearly stumbled over a still figure knelt beside the modest plot. Eliza remained transfixed though the others had long departed. Flower buds clung to her unbound hair and mud stained her frayed hem. But serenity smoothed her features as she contemplated death's raw disturbance of the living earth.

Quietly Ingram extended a hand to help her rise. "Come. Let us leave him to rest." Eliza obeyed, brushing dirt away. But her eyes retained their middle-distance gaze. Ingram felt words rise that must be spoken.

"I fear this land has become unsafe for your tender spirit," he began gently. "You endured such cruelty already. I cannot in conscience see you hazard more." He hesitated. "I may be able to arrange passage for you to a distant convent beyond Lord Ashcroft's reach."

He searched her downcast face. "You would be sheltered there to recover yourself fully. Please consider this escape I offer you."

Silence lingered between them on the path back to the village. Just as Ingram began despairing of any response, Eliza halted beneath the limbs of a flowering dogwood. She tilted her head up into the falling petals as if seeking answers from the sky.

"When I dwelled in darkness, I begged for just such refuge," she finally said. "To lay my head in some cloistered sanctuary far removed from worldly terror." Her grey eyes met Ingram's. "But now having known light again, I cannot hide away. There are souls trapped in shadow still. If I turn my back, their suffering continues unchecked."

Her delicate hands closed around Ingram's calloused ones. "You walk in hardship so others might endure. I would do the same." Resolve furrowed her brow. "We must stem this injustice, not flee it."

Pride and anxiety warred within Ingram. "The road ahead promises only greater peril," he warned reluctantly. "I cannot shield you from all harm."

"Nor should you." Eliza squeezed his hands firmly. "We are stronger together. My place is at your side now."

Ingram bowed his head, unable to resist her steadfast courage. She who had nearly succumbed to evil now became his stalwart ally. What destiny had forged their fates together? But divining providence's plan remained beyond mortal minds. Ingram could only walk onward and trust she would light the way as faithfully as he sought to guard her steps.

Side by side they continued down the dusty lane. The village's suffering weighed heavy, but resilient shoots of hope yet pushed through the rubble of despair. Together they would nourish those tender plants until life flourished anew. Though darkness amassed on the horizon, their shared light remained undimmed.

In the following days a pall hung over Bronwen's inn even as sunlight gradually leeched the gloom from its corners. Patrons still trickled in but spoke in murmurs and ate quickly before rushing out with eyes averted from the proprietress' raw grief. Bronwen herself moved numbly through her tasks, face etched with shadows no lamp could banish. Only young Aiken kept the business limping along, smiling bravely through red–rimmed eyes at each condolence as he tended the counter.

Ingram noted the change with growing unease. Trauma unleashed here would not remain confined to these stone walls. It seeped outward, poisoning hardy spirits and strengthening despair. Lord Ashcroft's cruel lesson proved more ruinous than the sword that dealt it. Fear now stalked where once camaraderie thrived.

On the fourth morning after the murder, Ingram approached Bronwen where she sat staring into chill hearth ashes. Gently he brushed her arm. She started as if woken from a nightmare. Seeing who disturbed her, Bronwen roughly knuckled away fresh tears.

"I beg your pardon," she muttered thickly. "Just woolgathering..."

"You have endured what no soul should," Ingram said simply. "But perhaps sitting idle only feeds darker thoughts." He gestured to her dusty apron and the room's clutter. "May I assist setting affairs in order? It is no burden, and the activity may do you good."

Bronwen hesitated, then ceded with a jerky nod. Ingram suppressed his relief—he had feared anything reminding her of former cheer would be met with fury or despair. But her spirit yet clung to life and purpose, though she knew it not. He prayed guiding her out of this abyss might restore the remarkable woman who had saved them all when they arrived battered and destitute.

Ingram let habit guide his tasks, scrubbing pots, sweeping ash, and beating dust from the straw ticking. Eliza joined him, mending torn chairs and curtains, hands busy but a deep empathy warming her delicate features. Around them Bronwen shuffled quietly, hesitantly at first, then gaining vigor. Simple directness focused her eyes and lifted the oppressive weight from her fragile bones.

By noon a semblance of order had returned to the common room, though its jovial warmth remained diminished. Still, Ingram was heartened to see faint sparks of life rekindling in Bronwen's vacant eyes. As she removed her apron and unbound her hair, the anguished and untethered soul seemed to steady. Ingram dared hope she had turned from the abyss staring back within.

Eliza approached with a bowl of stew and hunk of bread. "Please eat something now," she coaxed gently. When Bronwen accepted it, Eliza grasped her weathered hands. "You gave my spirit sanctuary though I was a stranger. Now let me aid you through this darkness in return."

The simple compassion cracked Bronwen's composure. Tears welling, she embraced Eliza with sudden desperation. They wept together, sharing an intimacy of profound loss that transcended any walls between them. Not every hurt could be mended, but even the act of binding wounds granted some small comfort.

At last, Bronwen released the girl, dabbing her damp cheeks and smiling weakly. "You have your father's kind heart," she murmured. "I was blessed indeed to know you both." Turning to include Ingram, she clasped their hands gratefully. The ghosts yet haunted her eyes, but hope flickered beneath their darkness.

Ingram tucked away the peculiar reference to Eliza's father for now. "I am glad to see you taking nourishment again. Strength of body will fortify your spirit." He gestured around the room. "Perhaps when you are able, we might prepare the tavern to reopen. These people need the light of community you kindled here."

Bronwen touched her temple wearily. "I cannot conjure the wherewithal just yet. But you speak truth." She nodded slowly. "Let us at least break bread together tonight. It would do Aiken good to see the tables full once more."

So, they supped solemnly that evening on pottage and ale, sharing subdued stories and grateful squeezes whenever grief swelled too sharply. They prepared a simple meal, to nourish souls gutted by loss. Though the food did not satisfy, the act of communal strength and care filled empty spaces. Ingram saw again how devastating evil was resisted through a thousand small acts of love.

Over the next few days, Bronwen roused herself to sweep the tavern porch and polish clouded windows. Candles were refreshed and a new cask of ale ventured up from the cellar. Bit by bit she edged back from the precipice though her eyes still strayed often to the town graveyard. But her son's memory would spur determination now rather than paralyze it.

The village remained wary, however. Patrons no longer lingered once fed. Nervous murmurs of relocating trailed in their wake. Ingram knew Lord Ashcroft's cruelty had fomented more violence to come. Fear begot brutality in a vicious cycle they must break. But Bronwen showed the only way was through courageous compassion, however fragile.

On an overcast morning, the bell over the door rang to announce a stooped laborer in rough spun wool. He shuffled to the bar looking uncomfortably out of place. When addressed, the taciturn man muttered a request for provisions to travel.

"Journeying somewhere?" Bronwen asked lightly, readying a parcel of hard bread and cheese.

The man shifted, avoiding her eye. "Aye, to...see to my sister. Taken suddenly ill."

Ingram observed the exchange from the doorway. The lie was plain. Before the man could bolt again, Ingram stepped forward and greeted him in a jovial tone that startled the skittish soul.

"Come, if your sister is sick surely Bronwen's cooking would do her well!" Opening the satchel, he pressed more cheese and a pot of honey beer into it. The man stared wide-eyed but found himself hustled to a table and presented with a bowl of stew.

"Now tell me of your kinfolk," Ingram prompted kindly, taking a seat himself. "I know something of the healing arts and may have knowledge to share."

The man glanced up apprehensively, sorrow clouding his eyes. "My apologies for my deception, sir. It was foolish of me. I just thought if you believed my sister was sick, you might be willing to spare some food and medicine before I leave this valley. Once I began the falsehood, I knew not how to undo it. I never meant any ill intent."

Ingram placed a gentle, forgiving hand on the man's slumped shoulder. "Times are hard for many folks now. While I wish you'd been truthful from the beginning, I cannot blame you for resorting to deception in your desperation." He sighed, meeting the man's gaze with understanding. "We must look out for one another. Stay a while and we will provide whatever provisions you need for the journey ahead."

The man's eyes widened, filling with grateful relief at Ingram's mercy. "Bless you for your kindness, sir! I surely will be in your debt."

A faint smile touched Ingram's lips. "There are no debts here between us...only a duty we all share to aid our fellow man in trying times." He beckoned the man to eat. "Now break bread with us. You must keep up your strength for the roads ahead." "You are wise to avoid what further darkness may come," he said gently. "But know that fear relinquishes this land to those forces. If you stay and help sow hope in your neighbors' hearts, that light may yet triumph."

Ingram gripped the man's hand. "Share that choice freely made with any whose path you cross. Here lie the seeds of lasting change."

Promising to reflect on these words, the man left with shoulders squared higher, parcel tucked under his arm. Ingram let him go with a prayer and smile. Not all could overcome ingrained terror to stay and resist. But through small acts, courage might spread.

Bronwen breathed deep as if a weight had lifted from her own spirit. Bustling to serve fresh pilgrims arrived, she shot Ingram a grateful look. "Your goodness shines ever brighter," she marveled, "no matter how deep the horrors you have faced."

Ingram ducked his head. "I merely reflect the light you and others have shared in my darkest hours." Glancing at the seat where the frightened man had found unexpected grace, he was reminded that none could predict how lost souls might find redemption in strange ways.

"If we can rekindle fading hopes, word will spread," he predicted. But Lord Ashcroft's long shadow yet lingered. Their trials had only begun.

Chapter Twenty

Over the following fortnight a few hearty souls returned to take evening meals at Bronwen's inn. Though familiar faces were conspicuously absent as many relocated from the valley rather than linger under the threat of Ashcroft's murderous knights. Fear ran too deep still, and Ingram did not fault any for choosing safety. But enough remained to prove this land would not surrender entirely.

On a sunny afternoon, Ingram stood in a clearing, splitting firewood with steady swings of an axe. Simon perched nearby trimming feathers for fresh fletching, brow knit in concentration as he shaped each quill. The youth still walked with a slight limp, but fresh vigor had returned to his bearing. Tempering his reckless passion with wisdom remained Ingram's hope. The humility of simple living was slowly leaving its mark on them both.

Eliza emerged from the inn wringing flour from her apron. Catching sight of Ingram, she smiled and approached the pile of split logs. "Shall I take some inside for the oven?" she asked, already gathering an armful of split oak.

Ingram lowered the axe, smiling faintly in return. "You needn't bother yourself with such menial labor. I'm happy to stock the room once I've finished."

Eliza made a bemused sound. "And I'm happy to help a dear friend so he doesn't chafe his back through exertion." Her eyes twinkled good-naturedly. "We all contribute however we can. Isn't that the very roots of community?"

Chastened by her gentle wisdom, Ingram surrendered with a chuckle and helped her carry enough wood for their immediate needs. The simple act of literally supporting one another lightened his spirit. Neither strength nor compassion flowed only one way. True bonds were forged through humility and service.

After stoking the oven's belly full, Eliza lingered by the hearth with hands spread as if soaking in its radiant warmth. The healthy glow in her cheeks testified to the restored vitality shining within. Ingram cherished this visible sign that her spirit had rebounded fully since it was nearly crushed in darkness. Each soul reclaimed from despair was a triumph and cause for hope.

Turning to Ingram, Eliza brushed back an errant hair, leaving a smudge of flour on her cheek. "What thoughts occupy you so deeply this fine day?" she inquired. "Your brow has been drawn with solemn contemplation all morning."

Ingram chuckled ruefully, both impressed by her perceptiveness and embarrassed at being so transparent. "Just restless notions and vague unease," he claimed. "I didn't mean for useless worry to show and dampen our refuge here."

Eliza tilted her head knowingly. "Come now. Your concerns do not stem from idleness, as I well know." She touched his arm. "Please unburden yourself. If I can share the weight, I shall."

Her earnest compassion broke through Ingram's reticence. Perching on the table's rough–hewn bench, he gathered his thoughts before speaking quietly.

"Though we have done our best, fear continues throttling the spirit of these people. And I cannot shake a dark premonition that Lord Ashcroft will soon strike again." He stared into the flickering hearth; brow furrowed. "Have I brought more harm than help with my presence? Perhaps we should move on before violence returns."

Eliza considered his words for a thoughtful moment. "Light will always draw darkness in its jealousy," she finally replied. "But does that mean we should hide our lamps away for fear of shadows?"

She shook her head firmly. "What befell this village would have come regardless. At least we helped sow seeds of resilience." Taking Ingram's calloused hands, Eliza held his gaze. "The only mistake would be leaving before they yield fruit. Stay the course, have faith."

Her steadfast wisdom stirred shame at his own doubts. Eliza had endured profound darkness yet emerged with compassion undimmed. Would he do any less?

"Your counsel is just," Ingram acknowledged, squeezing her delicate hands. "We shall abide here until these people stand strong together again or perish in the attempt."

A heavy knock suddenly shook the timbers, startling them apart. Exchanging a quick glance, they moved to peer cautiously out. Bronwen stood in the yard speaking with an old man swathed in a rough hooded cloak despite the mild weather. Urgent hands emphasized his hushed words.

Sensing trouble, Ingram stepped outside. "Is all well here?" he inquired calmly.

Bronwen turned to him, features creased with concern. "Tomas here bears grim tidings from the valley. Go on," she prompted the old man.

Trembling, he related dire proclamations issued by Lord Ashcroft. A fortnight remained for all farmers and merchants to deliver triple tithes or forfeit their lands and goods. Ashcroft blamed lean harvests and lagging trade on peasant sloth rather than the turmoil inflicted by his cruelty. Any unable to pay would be deemed outlaws without sanctuary or quarter.

Ingram's throat tightened at the injustice, but he kept his voice steady. "Does anyone else know of these heinous decrees?"

The old man shook his hooded head sadly. "I left straight away once the messengers began pounding on doors with writs of taxation. The others are cowering behind barred windows and shuttered lamps. None will have the courage to resist or spread word."

He clasped Ingram's arm. "But you all showed bravery against the soldiers. Surely you won't let that dog Ashcroft drive us from our rightful homes?" Desperation shone in his eyes.

Ingram chose his response carefully. "No petty tyrant can stand long when confronted by righteous souls united for justice." He gripped the old man's shoulder. "Rouse what brave hearts remain, and we shall forge a peace beyond tyranny's reach."

The elder peered at Ingram intently, then shuffled off with new vigor in his gait. Ingram watched him depart with turmoil roiling beneath his calm expression. Events were spiraling beyond control before he could cement unity here. And directly challenging Ashcroft's knights invited bloody ruin. To defend the innocent, Ingram's own hands must again take up violence. The thought turned his spirit cold despite the justness of their cause.

Eliza slipped a soft hand into his, sensing his inner conflict. "You offer them the only hope against oppression," she murmured. "Have faith their courage and your light shall lead the way."

Bronwen approached, worry lines etched deep. "Tomas speaks true. Word is spreading that Ashcroft means to wring this land dry." She wrung her hands helplessly. "But what can a handful of poor farmers do against armored men?"

Ingram faced both women resolutely. "They need not stand alone. I swear to you both, I shall not let this injustice go uncontested." He gestured to Simon who had approached nearby. "We three will take word of Ashcroft's cruelty and corruption to my order across the mountains. Allies will return with us to enfranchise these people."

Bronwen looked doubtful but heartened by his confidence. She had witnessed enough of Ingram's valor to trust him implicitly. "I had better warn Aiken to lay up extra stores here if we're to harbor rebellion." She grasped Ingram's hands firmly. "God speed you on this journey. But return safely, I beg of you."

Ingram clasped her shoulder. "The light will endure. Keep it kindled in people's hearts until we come again."

Bronwen nodded firmly before withdrawing inside to share the solemn tidings with Aiken. Ingram turned to find Eliza regarding him intently. "You plan to petition your order for assistance?" she asked. "Will they aid unknown peasants against a lord of the realm?"

Ingram hesitated. Much remained unexplained regarding his tangled history with Ashcroft and the nature of his crusade. But Eliza deserved truth, however bitter.

"I shall petition my former commander to reprimand his wayward son," he admitted. At her startled look Ingram continued reluctantly. "Lord Ashcroft's father Maxwell is master of my old order pledged to fight corruption and darkness. If he learns his heir's depravity firsthand, we shall have potent allies against injustice."

Eliza studied his pained expression, understanding dawning in her eyes. "You feel reluctance given your past allegiance? Do not let old loyalties cloud what must be done for right."

She touched his cheek gently. "Stay true on the path ahead. I know your heart remains virtuous."

Her unwavering faith kindled Ingram's courage. For her sake and the oppressed people here, he would conquer whatever lingering doubts and ghosts from the past. Evil must be met with swift justice wherever it arose. He only prayed his brothers would recognize Ashcroft's cruelty demanded stern correction, not mercy.

Ingram departed on a strong steed at dusk well provisioned by Bronwen. Eliza and Simon accompanied him on mares along the forest trail. They went along until the valley cradling the village disappeared. Wooded ridges rose steadily toward the peaks dividing this shire from Ingram's homeland. There Simon and Eliza bade him a solemn farewell before riding back to help maintain the flickering lamp of hope. Ingram faced the mountain pass, channeling his unease into resolve. The cold wind keened through bluffs centuries old, reminding him that evil persevered as long as good folk stood idle. But no longer. He would rally the righteous and guide them back as liberators. Justice would prevail.

The frosted peaks brooded in silence as Ingram bent his steps eastward.

Chapter Twenty-One

Ingram leaned into the wind as his steed coursed through the exposed mountain pass. Hunched against the chill in a sheepskin hooded cloak, he rode over the icy stone trail worn shallow by centuries of traders and shepherds. Behind him, the remote valley and its beleaguered residents receded into cloud-shrouded shadow. Ahead lay the unknown reception waiting at journey's end.

When he crested the windswept saddle between jagged peaks, Ingram halted briefly to regain bearings and respite. Across a deep chasm reared an even greater snow-mantled spur speckled with twisted pines. That rocky spine marked the edge of his one-time homeland. Somewhere within that cold fastness stood the ancient stronghold, housing the ascetic order pledged to combating evil and injustice across the land.

Ingram had not laid eyes on the fortress sanctuary since the day his world shattered. Even gazing upon its mountain bulwark caused fresh pain to pierce his battle-worn heart. For in those halls, he had trained with hand and spirit to fight wickedness, only to discover corruption festering unchecked within. The bitter irony still stung. But duty compelled him to bear these ghosts. Too much depended on the order's potent allies joining Ingram's crusade against the merciless Lord Ashcroft.

With the sun dipping below the jagged ridgeline, Ingram pressed on toward the tree line. Dark memories haunted the deep woods, but he steeled himself and rode until the gnarled trunks swallowed him from sight. The trees here had witnessed his greatest shame those many seasons past. But just as their roots weathered the years, he endured as well. Wiser, wearier, and perhaps less blinded by arrogant ideals. He could only trust that the intervening time had also granted perspective to those in power.

As night enfolded the silent forest, old instincts took over to guide Ingram along the faint trail. Adrenaline tingled his senses, every snapping twig seeming a potential threat as encroaching darkness summoned primal terrors. But no arrow greeted him from the undergrowth, and no black forms stirred between the firs to harry his passage. The sworn protectors haunted these reaches only in his memory now. All flesh and blood survivors had long ago scattered to the winds.

Without warning, the dense wood opened into a clearing bathed in filtered moonlight. Mist clung to the ground, pooling thickest around a ring of megaliths etched with dire runes. This ancient site had remained outside the order's domain, untouched for ages before Ingram violated its sanctity. He shivered with more than the icy caress of hidden specters. Every choice that fateful night had left scars on his own soul and the land itself. No simple quest for aid could erase such wrongs.

Hesitating at the forest verge, Ingram drew his cloak tight against the chill seeping into his bones. "If any restless spirits linger, I come in humility to make amends," he rasped aloud. Only the sigh of night winds answered. Ingram bowed his head prayerfully before continuing on haunted ground. The past could be neither changed nor outrun. But present courage might transform its bitter legacy.

Head down as if traveling into the teeth of a gale, Ingram circled wide around the weathered monoliths. Forgotten voices clamored on the edge of hearing, threading foreboding through the stillness. He dared not lift his eyes to pierce the veil and glimpse whatever shadows still clung to this desecrated site. The breath of the grave lapped icy against his neck during the brief tortured span before dense forest swallowed him again. Exhaling raggedly, Ingram hurried onward as if being chased by phantoms.

As a recruit he had flown along this trail, chasing his comrades in boisterous games to pass the time patrolling their domain. Now only penitent purpose carried him along the final painful mile.

Rounding a bend, the trees fell away to reveal sloping lawns and cultivated terraces surrounding the bastion of his former order. Turrets and parapets stood etched against the cold vault of stars, still anchoring the mountains against encroaching darkness. A beacon pyre atop the gatehouse tower lent the only spot of warmth and color. Ingram stood haloed in that lambent glow, irrationally hesitant to approach even this familiar refuge. But the deed must be done, no matter the personal cost in reflected shame.

Steeling himself, Ingram dismounted and marched up to the iron-banded portal and seized the hanging chain to bang the ancient clapper. The dull booming echoed within the vaulted entry tunnel. Ingram counted the tolls dying away into expectant silence. At the count of ten, a small viewing grate slid open, and a pair of wary eyes peered out. Recognition flickered in their depths before the guard's gruff voice issued a challenge.

"State your name and allegiance, night-skulker."

Ingram drew himself erect, gazing steadily into his past. "I am called Ingram of Gault, former sergeant sworn to this order. I come seeking counsel with Maxwell Ashcroft by right of past service."

The studying eyes blinked in surprise, but the sentry quickly recovered protocol. "None pass at night without the master's blessing. You must bide here until dawn if your claims be true." With that he slid the grate shut, leaving Ingram alone in the small circle of torchlight beyond the wall.

Accepting this expected prudence, Ingram pulled his cloak tighter and found what minimal shelter he could in the gate tunnel. Sleep would be elusive with anticipation twisting his stomach. But he must enter the audience rested in body and spirit. The dawn would reveal if Ingram still had any brothers within these walls.

The morning sun crested the battlements to spear Ingram's closed eyes where he sat propped against cold stone. Grimacing, he rose to stamp circulation back into his numb extremities. He felt twice his thirty winters after the long journey and sleepless vigil. But such trials were forgotten entering the presence of past heroes.

Heavy footfalls presaged the grate sliding open again. This time the guard nodded brusquely. "Come. Master Maxwell will grant you audience."

Ingram murmured thanks and followed the guard through the imposing gates and into torchlit halls he had never thought to walk again. Unfamiliar monks eyed him sidelong on his way to the audience chamber. His escort's presence and Ingram's lack of any visible weapon seemed the only reasons he wasn't surrounded with naked steel. The hostility simmering beneath their circumspect reserve left no doubt; he returned to this sanctum as much a stranger as prodigal son.

At last, they ascended the worn steps to the solar overlooking the valley pass. Morning sun streamed through arched windows, framing a long table where places had been set for the order's leadership. But only one hooded figure stood silhouetted against the light—the aged but still vigorous form of Maxwell Ashcroft, master and founder of this crusade against the forces of darkness.

Ingram approached slowly, halting at a respectful distance until addressed. Maxwell turned, the sunlight etching deep lines of care and authority into his rugged features. Keen eyes like polished flint swept over Ingram in close assessment. Recognition sparked, but no hint of the resentment Ingram had steeled himself against.

"Ingram of Gault," Maxwell rumbled. "It has been some years since any sheltered here saw your face." He beckoned toward the laden table. "Come. Share bread and ale, and we shall discuss what urgent need brings you unannounced to my hall."

Unsure what to make of his mild reception, Ingram took the indicated chair. He bit into a crusty heel of bread to grant time to order swirling thoughts. Maxwell studied him openly as he ate. Ingram noted the master's once sable locks had faded to iron, and care seemed to etch fresh lines daily across his brow. But strength yet inhabited his imposing frame, and wisdom lingered in his piercing gaze.

Seeing Ingram had finished, Maxwell folded his hands expectantly. "I discern heavy tidings weigh upon your spirit. Unburden yourself, and by God's grace we shall determine what course to set."

Ingram set down his emptied mug, jaw tightening. "I thank you for the fair hearing, as I have no right to ask it." Taking a breath, he continued. "I bring grave news of your son Ashcroft's deeds across the border. He rules his lands with cruelty, demanding ruinous tithes while inflicting brutal reprisals against any dissent. His knights terrorize the peasants, destroying lives over the least offense."

Ingram held Maxwell's stoic gaze. "I witnessed a woman's child murdered before her simply to teach submission. Such horrific injustice stains your own legacy. I beseech you, send aid before all is drowned in blood."

Silence engulfed the solar as Ingram's damning report faded. Maxwell stared into the middle distance, his craggy features graven from stone. Ingram braced himself for dismissal or outrage at the implicit criticism of flesh and blood. But he had sworn to give full accounting. The rest lay in heaven's hands.

At long last Maxwell sighed heavily, seeming to age a dozen years before Ingram's eyes. "Dire accusations indeed," he intoned wearily. "And if even a fraction be accurate, the situation demands correction." He passed a broad hand over his eyes before pinning Ingram with a piercing look.

"Might other factors have ignited your personal feud with my heir? I remember well your... history together." Maxwell raised a forestalling hand against Ingram's protest. "I imply no deceit, only that passion can obscure perspective."

Ingram drew a calming breath. "My own past actions may render me undeserving of trust," he allowed. "But a community of innocents now suffers unjustly. I ask only that you verify these charges yourself before more unjust blood is spilled." He held Maxwell's astute gaze. "If Lord Winton Ashcroft is innocent, I will surrender myself to your judgment for my transgressions."

Maxwell absorbed this calmly, nodding to himself. "Your offer speaks well of your character. Very well." He rose, clasping Ingram's shoulder firmly. "I shall lead a troop across the border on the morrow. Pray God this is but some misunderstanding, not irredeemable rot within my house."

Ingram rose swiftly, overwhelmed that Maxwell believed him enough to investigate personally. "I lack any gift to repay this leap of faith, except my own humble service now and ever." He bowed his head, afraid to trust that full reconciliation may come in time.

A heavy hand rested gently upon Ingram's bent neck. "Peace, lad. You were as a son to me once, before fate drove us apart." Maxwell's tone held great sadness, but also hope of redemption. "I pray now we walk again in shared light against darkness."

Emotion choked Ingram's voice. "From your lips to heaven's ears."

Chapter Twenty-Two

Over the next day, Ingram furnished Maxwell with further details on Ashcroft's depravities to guide the knights' mission. Though he longed to strike out immediately to the oppressed valley, he would only hinder their cause by arriving ahead of Maxwell's authority. Patience and faith must guide his feet along redemption's thorny path.

So, Ingram waited in contemplative solitude, haunting the battlements overlooking the winding mountain trails once so familiar. He felt the accusatory glares of monks who marked his bruised and branded exile from this sanctum. Ingram ignored their silent censure, just as he turned aside memories haunted by shameful failures. The past could no longer fetter his resolute steps toward justice and brotherhood regained.

On the second day, horns sounded from the gatehouse turrets signaling Maxwell's departure with his retinue of knights. Ingram stood vigil until the trailing dust settled beyond sight around a bend in the deep gorge. He offered ardent prayers for their mission and swift return. If their charges held true, a fearsome reckoning awaited the cruel lord of these borderlands. For the first time in years, Ingram felt the stirrings of a profound peace. Whatever came, he had opened his heart and spoken truth. The rest lay beyond his mortal hands.

Despite the intervening miles, Ingram felt linked to those riding forth by bonds of shared purpose. He had planted the seed of hope. Now it fell to brave souls to tend the sprout and help scatter its nourishing fruit abroad. Together they would sow the seeds of justice and reap the promise of redemption.

The waiting days passed slowly as Ingram kept vigil for any sign of Maxwell's return. He ventured deep into the surrounding woods to gather fresh charcoal and herbs, losing himself for precious hours in menial tasks. Anything to still his racing thoughts and channel nervous energy into routine. He avoided the guarded scrutiny of the monks in their bustling compound, just as they gave him a wide berth. But occasionally a shared glance acknowledged their common hopes for resolution without further bloodshed.

At night Ingram retreated to an isolated parapet to meditate beneath the wheeling stars. He was tracing familiar constellations one cloudless eve when approaching footsteps drew his attention. A silhouette paused at the top of the worn steps, face obscured but bearing unmistakably that of the master. Ingram surged to his feet.

"You have returned. What news?" He searched Maxwell's shadowed features, dread coiling at the prolonged silence. Had Ashcroft's snakes unleashed even greater chaos upon the oppressed people?

The master stepped into a bar of moonlight, features grim beneath his drawn hood. "We found troubling truths awaiting in the border valleys," he confirmed heavily. "My son has gravely overstepped authority there."

Ingram released a slow breath. Then Maxwell's use of the present tense registered fully. He tensed. "You speak as if Lord Ashcroft yet rules. Did you not justly remove him from influence?"

Maxwell held up a staying hand. "Peace. We confronted him in the abbey you described. He resisted authority but has now been placed under guard and bound for trial." He sighed deeply. "But it seems whispers of chaos reach other ears. Renegade knights attacked our party this eve as we withdrew."

Ingram's chest tightened. "Your men...?"

"Scattered, though some were gravely injured. We became separated in the skirmish." Maxwell's face creased with sorrow. "They know these lands better and mean to ambush us piecemeal."

Ingram turned aside, gripping the rough parapet. Treachery still abounded, threatening everything. "We should gather your knights immediately before Ashcroft loyalist can overwhelm us."

Maxwell shook his head grimly. "Our numbers would only breed chaos and mistrust. I alone must finish this pilgrimage."

He clasped Ingram's shoulder meaningfully. "Escort my prisoner back to face justice. Then return with aid for these people until stability is restored." His stern face softened slightly. "No matter what befalls, have faith."

Before Ingram could respond, the master turned and descended swiftly into darkness. Stunned by this sudden burden of responsibility, Ingram nevertheless trusted Maxwell's wisdom. He would not fail these people again. After a steadying moment of prayer, he made his way swiftly toward the cells below. There lay the seeds of lasting change. He need only remain faithful.

The pale light of false dawn crept through barred windows lining the dank passage. Ingram nodded to the guards and examined the placed lock and blessed fetters binding the cell's sole occupant. Ashcroft looked paler after days confined in shadow. But cunning remained sharp in his hollow eyes as he took in this unexpected visit.

"So, they send a dog to escort me," he sneered. "How righteous when your own hands are stained."

Ingram remained unmoved. "I come at your father's behest to ensure justice." He turned to his taciturn escort. "Ready your swiftest steeds. We leave as soon as I take charge of the prisoner."

The guards hurried to obey. Alone now, Ingram faced the chained Ashcroft. "Whatever your past crimes, repent and find redemption." He shook his head sadly. "It is not too late for light to reclaim your darkened soul."

Ashcroft threw back his head and laughed harshly. "Preach to these fools if you wish. I know your true heart, Ingram." His sunken eyes glinted as he raised his shackled wrists. "We are brethren bound by blood. This changes nothing."

Ingram stepped closer, expression hardening. "It can. This is a final chance to throw off evil's yoke before its fire consumes you." He searched Ashcroft's face for any shred of remorse. "Renounce wickedness, then aid these people to heal."

For a flickering instant indecision touched the disgraced lord's features. But then his mouth twisted in a vicious sneer. "Keep your naïve pieties. I remain master of my domain." He leaned closer, breath hot and voice dropping ominously. "You cannot fathom the true power I now wield."

Suppressing a chill, Ingram drew away. "Very well. You choose your own path." He turned at approaching footsteps. The guards had returned silently leading a saddled charger and pack mule. Ingram took up the prisoner's chains to lead him into dim morning light and whatever justice awaited.

The knights flanked Ingram and Ashcroft as their small company descended the twisting mountain track. Ingram kept vigilant for ambush, but the surrounding woods remained eerily still except for the sigh of wind. Perhaps renegade factions yet awaited them on the border itself. But Ingram took heart that he had regained lost brothers to continue defending the innocent. Together they would brighten that oppressed land.

When the terrain leveled near midday, Ingram called a brief halt to rest the animals and take frugal meals. He parted reluctantly with a portion of bread and dried meat for the chained Ashcroft. Whatever seeds of goodness might remain in his corrupted soul, Ingram would try to nurture them. Perhaps in time light would overcome spite.

Remounting to continue their descent, Ingram's thoughts dwelled on Eliza and the community awaiting deliverance. He prayed they had the strength for a few more days until support arrived. Each step carried him back to aiding their resilient hope. Light seared deepest shadows when kindled in courageous hearts united by love. If he clung to that truth, doubt could not long endure.

The wooded foothills gave way to mist–shrouded meadows and tilled fields silvered by late sun. A lone cowherd gaped at their grim procession before fleeing into the billowing fog. Ingram's unease stirred. Such abandoned pastures should be teeming on the warm summer eve. Where had all souls fled to in fear?

Topping a final rise, the valley cradling Bronwen's village opened before them. Dark fumes blotted the sky above thatched roofs. Raucous laughter and coarse shouts drifted as armored brutes dragged struggling forms from smoldering cottages. The grassy ways now ran red beneath iron-shod hooves. Ingram froze at this nightmare made real once again. Their world aflame while he tarried blindly leagues away, deaf to these people's cries.

Ashcroft's grating chuckle broke his horrified trance. "You see the price of defiance?" His chains rattled as he leaned close. "I promised they would suffer worse for sheltering you, heretic."

Ingram turned slowly to face his smirking captive fury overpowering shock. This desecration could not stand. He had sworn to protect these people yet led threat straight to their door. But there was still time to purge this filth from the valley.

Unleashing his cold wrath, Ingram struck Ashcroft across the jaw, snapping his head back viciously. "You will burn for this," Ingram swore, drawing his stunned knights close. "But by heaven's light, not hell's!"

Turning his charger toward the burning village, Ingram tore his holy crest from concealment and raised it high. "With me, brothers! Justice this day!"

Chapter Twenty-Three

Spurring his mount forward, Ingram thundered down the slope with the knights galloping behind. Fury kindled his blood at the wanton brutality staining the valley below. Innocence had flowered here briefly between shadowed peaks before Ashcroft's poisoned malice trampled their fragile shoot. No more—that desecration ended today.

Ingram roared wrath as he crashed into the ravaged village, sword cleaving towards the first dazed brute. Brief surprise froze the pillagers, but instinct quickly hardened their faces with ruthless purpose. Soldiers converged to intercept these reckless interlopers, serrated blades thirsty for fresh blood.

With a clash of steel, the forces collided in a savage frenzy. Training honed in the order's unforgiving drills held Ingram and the knights in good stead as they battled without mercy. Screams of the wounded fed fury as Ingram cut down any thug bold or foolish enough to close within his whirling blade's reach.

But the tide turned as roused venom surged through the bloodied streets. Claws seemed to pierce Ingram from behind while a spear point glanced off his shoulder pauldron. Reeling in the saddle, Ingram swung wild strikes to force space. The alley had become a visceral nightmare. A gauntleted fist crashed into his temple, toppling Ingram from his panicking horse into the mud churned by warring feet.

Dazed, Ingram tried to stand and was kicked brutally down. Laughing faces leered through slit helms as steel tips prodded his exposed vitals. Ingram tensed for the ending blow, bitterly regretting this reckless charge. Around him lay strewn the monks who followed him so trustingly into ruin, along with innocents whose desperate cries yet echoed from broken homes.

He had failed them all.

A strangled shout drew Ingram's lolling gaze upward. The press of soldiers abruptly parted as a bloodied figure staggered into view. Lord Ashcroft clutched his throat, crimson welling around the bolt buried deep. His sunken eyes landed on Ingram, widened in shock and mortal agony. Then Ashcroft collapsed face-first to the muck, limbs twitching weakly before lying still.

Howls of outrage went up as Ashcroft's minions swarmed over their fallen master. Ingram gaped in numb disbelief from his own rank vantage. The tyrant who orchestrated this butchery had been felled by...what? Ingram had not even noted the missile amidst the chaos, but perhaps one villager escaped massacre to exact fatal vengeance.

Ashcroft was slain. Leaderless, his rabble would surely scatter without organized purpose. Ingram might have rejoiced were his own prospects not so bleak. There would be no mercy for the one who brought an army down on them. He twisted against ungentle grips, searching for some improbable escape. If he could reach the horses, outrun them...

A bugle's brash notes sliced through barked commands, silencing all. The mud-slicked mob parted as a ring of marching pikemen closed in, steel tips forming an impenetrable thicket.

In their midst strode a lordly figure in ceremonial armor, stained cloak of rank flowing. Ingram's heart seized as the noble pushed past gawking minions to stand imperiously over Ashcroft's corpse. Grief marred the lined face beneath neatly oiled hair. This could only be...

"Father," Ingram rasped through bloodied lips. "You are unharmed."

Maxwell Ashcroft's stern gaze found Ingram. To his shock, a sad smile briefly lifted the weathered cheeks. "Well met, my wayward son. Though much has gone awry." He shook his cloaked head at the body leaking into the mud. "Would that we were rejoined in more hopeful times."

Turning to address his encircling men, Maxwell proclaimed in a voice echoing off broken walls, "This stain upon my lineage ends today. See the fallen bound for cleansing rites." He swept an imperious hand. "Confine all their wicked flock for judgment."

Disciplined pikemen swiftly disarmed Ingram's captors and bound them for processing. Ingram sagged, strength bleeding out through his wounds now that desperation no longer fueled each breath. As consciousness wavered, he glimpsed Maxwell gazing down upon him, his expression unreadable. Ingram tried to shape grateful words, to articulate through cracked lips how destiny had woven their fates together against all odds. But darkness swallowed his vision before speech took form.

When awareness returned, Ingram found himself lying on fresh hay in an unfamiliar peasant hut. Footsteps approached, accompanied by the clink of glass vials. A tonsured monk with healer's garb and kind eyes knelt to apply pungent unguents to Ingram's bandaged wounds. The sting helped banish woolen-headed sensation left by potent sedatives.

"Be still," the monk soothed. "Your body remains badly damaged, but the inner fire yet shines. Rest and let my herbs aid your mending."

Ingram nodded weakly, lacking even the strength to voice questions swirling through his sluggish thoughts. How had the righteous prevailed? What fate befell those he had sworn to protect? As darkness reclaimed his exhausted mind, Ingram clung desperately to faith that some purpose endured beyond suffering.

When next he woke clear-headed, Ingram found Simon sitting vigil at his bedside. The youth sprang up as Ingram tried to shift his aching body.

"Praise God, you are alive!" Simon exclaimed, clasping Ingram's hand warmly. "We despaired as fever wracked you these long days."

Ingram gripped him back firmly, voice a ragged ruin. "Eliza...the villagers...?"

"They are well, my friend, thanks to your brave foolishness." Affection and exasperation vied in Simon's tone. "You must rest and regain strength. Then all shall be explained."

Too weak to resist, Ingram surrendered to the herbal draughts spooned between his parched lips. Healing dreams embraced him, soothing the memory of frantic violence. Divine purpose yet guided all in mysterious ways. If he had faith, understanding would illuminate his path once more. For now, dreamless rest knit bone and sinew under dedicated care. Healing must begin from within.

The passage of days marked by warmth and comfort slowly restored Ingram's depleted reserves. Mindful of his still mending wounds, Eliza and Bronwen extended loving succor while Simon related events following Ingram's desperate ride into the valley. Much yet required reconciliation, but evil had been purged from this sanctuary. Now began the holier work of forging peace in its wake.

When Ingram could finally rise with assistance and hobble outside, brilliant sunlight reflected his own heart soaring at life's persistence. Throughout the village, able men and women toiled mending broken walls and spirits. Laughter warmed the air as children darted about underfoot, blessedly oblivious to lingering hardship. Though scarred and weary, these people endured to welcome a new dawn.

Supported between Eliza and Simon, Ingram walked slowly amidst signs of healing. Bronwen hastened over, face lined from fresh grief but eyes alight to see Ingram upright. She clasped his hands warmly.

"Bless you, son. Once more you brought us deliverance." Glancing around her restored tavern yard, she shook her head in wonder. "Had I not witnessed it myself, I'd scarce believe such goodness yet walked this earth."

Ingram ducked his head. "I only give form to the light already shining within you all." He gestured to Eliza and Simon. "Together we kindle enough hope to route any darkness."

A gentle cough drew their eyes to where a lordly man stood leaning on a simple staff as he observed the bustling villagers. Ingram straightened reflexively before the measured stare he had known since childhood.

"Greetings, Ingram. It heartens me to see you mended." Maxwell Ashcroft clasped his shoulder with calloused warmth. "I wished to speak once unrest here was calmed. Will you walk with me?"

Ingram glanced at his anxious friends, then nodded. "Of course, Mas—" He caught himself. "Father."

Escorting his shuffling steps, Maxwell guided them to a humble cemetery on the village outskirts. There amongst the rough-hewn stones, a freshly turned plot marked the corrupted son's final rest. Ingram stared at the raw earth, words failing him.

"We commit his twisted body and soul to God's judgment." Maxwell's voice carried the hollowness of lessons learned too late. "His evil shall shadow my spirit until it too finds peace." The master sighed heavily, seeming to age before Ingram's eyes. "I failed you both as a teacher and father."

Ingram clasped the older man's slumped shoulders. "The fault lies with me. I strayed from the righteous path, poisoned by pride." He met Maxwell's questioning look. "But your lessons finally took root. Because you planted goodness in my heart, I could withstand darkness until finding light again."

As the master's eyes shone with gratitude, Ingram felt the cold brand of exile finally lift from his soul. Their wayward family had overcome hate with love. From this reconciliation, a new covenant would arise.

Side by side, they walked back into the radiant village ready to bind up lingering wounds. Whatever the future held, Ingram knew he would not face it alone. Bonds of faith now anchored him against fear and doubt. Darkness inevitably fell, but their shared light would ever pierce it.

Don't miss out!

Visit the website below and you can sign up to receive emails whenever Ken Sandoval publishes a new book. There's no charge and no obligation.

https://books2read.com/r/B-A-MUCV-GWQDD

BOOKS 2 READ

Connecting independent readers to independent writers.

Also by Ken Sandoval

The Guardians
Crimson Harvest